THE DRAGON'S VOW

SILVER DRAGON SHIFTER BROTHERS 3

MARIE JOHNSTON

LE PUBLISHING

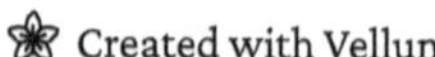 Created with Vellum

Steel

When my brother was busy trying to win the mate of his dreams, I may have indulged a time or twenty in the voluptuous curves of a human woman. I fell hard and when I asked her for more, she turned me down flat. She would never move to the small shifter town I lived in and I could never leave. Message received. So I walked away before I told her what I was. Then I find out she's pregnant with my young.

Avril

I moved to a big city after high school and I've been savoring the anonymity ever since. Then Steel shows up and destroys the tidy but exhausting life I've built for myself. I'm not allowed to raise a dragon shifter kid away from the clan, and since I know Steel's shifter secret, I have to mate him. So, basically, I'm losing everything I worked for. But I refuse to lose my heart, no matter what.

CHAPTER
ONE

S teel

I WAS HARD AGAIN. Painfully erect and throbbing. It was my perpetual state since I had come back from Minnesota. Lying in bed and staring at the ceiling while my body raged like I was a rutting stud fenced off from a pasture of fertile mares was becoming a new pastime. A pathetic one, but there it was.

The worst part was I had no one to talk to. I couldn't tell my brothers. They'd oscillate between demanding to know what I'd been thinking and pity for the condition I was left in. A guy didn't go up to his brother and ask, *Do you know how badly unrequited sucks?* Dragon shifters didn't do that, and I wasn't just any dragon shifter.

I was Steel Silver. An unfortunate name, but there it was. It was like my parents wanted to enforce that I wasn't just second-in-command, I was an unyielding second-in-command. Good luck breaking me to get to my oldest brother, the overseer of all dragon shifters.

And now I was the only single Silver brother. Deacon was deliriously happy with his human mate Ava, and my youngest brother Penn mated with Venus, the youngest of the ruling family of Jade clan. Deacon had barely cleared the deadline of thirty-fifth birthday before he got mated, but Penn wasn't yet twenty-six. My thirty-fifth birthday was over two years away. I didn't need to rush to find a mate, but that didn't mean I didn't want to.

That didn't mean I hadn't met someone, and that she hadn't shut me down hard.

We can't tell anybody about this.

It was just a fling, you know that, right?

I've got to get my life back on track. I've got to think about me.

It figured—I had met someone, and she didn't want me. I'd never had an issue with females. If I wanted to get laid, I did. There were a few females from the clan that I'd met with regularly. Females who waited for true love to strike before they turned thirty-five. Females I hoped had better luck than me.

The reason I was painfully erect didn't feel the same way about me. She didn't want me long term. At some point, I should get over her.

Right?

Whatever point that was, I hadn't reached it yet, and it'd been two months.

With a groan, I rolled out of bed and trudged toward the shower. The cool wooden floor of my remodeled early 1900s farmhouse creaked under my feet. I turned the antique knob of the wooden door to the bathroom and stepped straight into the shower before I turned the water on. There was no need to bother with hot water this morning.

The only benefit of not being able to get her off my mind was a lower hot water bill.

I palmed my erection and let the cold water splatter my face and chest. Shivers erupted over my skin, and a grimace drew my lips off my teeth. I pumped through the frigid shock and let my imagination run wild since it was all I had.

Long brown hair caressing the tips of full, round breasts. Reddish-pink nipples bouncing in front of my face. Lush round hips and thick thighs that I had gotten lost in for hours.

Goddamn, it didn't take long.

I hit my climax in record time and ignored where my release sprayed. I'd wash myself and clean up after I relieved some of the pressure. I'd probably end up jacking off again before the shower was done. That was how bad of shape I was in.

After my new morning routine was done, I dried off and got dressed. My black police uniform was for show only. On paper, I was a Silver Lake police officer. A rarity for a town this small to have one lone cop, but common for places where shifter clans resided.

I even carried a gun in a holster at my hip. Shifters didn't use weapons—except for the unfortunate situation that happened in Garnet River a couple months ago. The results should've set an example. Everyone who'd used a gun against shifters was dead. All but one and someone else called dibs on ending his life. Hunting rifles were for hunting, not trying to take control of a clan.

If a shifter wanted to do that, they had to use their teeth and claws and fighting ability like nature intended.

I grabbed a premade bacon-and-cheese bagel from the fridge and tossed it into the microwave. My brothers joked about my meal prep, but they reaped the benefits when they came to visit. Their visits had dwindled, and I'd had to adjust my food buying—and my tolerance of loneliness.

While my bagel heated, I leaned against the counter and closed my eyes. Sleep had been shit for two months. I didn't understand it. I could see the increased masturbation and the surprise erections throughout the day, but the restless sleep? I had to be tired on top of being heartbroken?

You see your brothers getting married. It's nostalgia or something. Maybe FOMO? This isn't real, Steel. This is just two lonely people ignoring what's really wrong.

According to her, what was really wrong was that she needed to be comfortable with herself. And she hated small towns. I couldn't leave Silver Lake, and she refused to move here. We hadn't even reached that problem. She had shut me down before then.

I let out a gusty sigh.

It wasn't just the sleep either. I'd had a general sense of restlessness since I had returned to Silver Lake. Like I needed to be with her when she was the one person in my life who told me to go away.

For fuck's sake. I was a walking pity party. I could turn into a damn dragon, but I couldn't quit moping over a girl. It was like I cut my balls off and made her earrings before I left.

The microwave dinged. I pulled my food out, not caring that it burned the tips of my fingers. I healed fast. Wrapping it in a paper towel, I took a bite and carried it with me as I locked up the house and went to the pickup.

I was meeting Deacon at city hall. The drive only took two minutes. After I was done meeting with him, I would patrol city limits and then work my way out from there.

Silver Lake was named after both my family and the big lake on my family's property—officially Deacon's property. Silver Lake had less than a thousand people, all shifters or their human mates. Some of our clan lived and worked in Wildrose, not far away. Jade Hills was less than a half hour away in another direction. We blended into the area of the Turtle Mountains. Families who'd forever hidden a major secret.

Deacon ruled Silver clan as the mayor on paper for nosy humans. I was the cop, and Penn was a scholar, now setting up online educational systems for all the clans from his home in Jade Hills.

The most important part of my position was being seen. To let our clan know we cared about their safety. Being the second brother, the underling, my role was still to act partly as a politician. On the security side, I intervened in any issues and protected my brothers.

That had been enough for me—secure and protect. Shake a few hands and hand out some candy during the summer parade. Until two months ago when I had entertained the idea of more.

Fuck, I needed to get over her.

I wished it was as easy as going to the bar and finding someone to have sex with. I hadn't entertained the thought since I'd returned. A naive part of me I hadn't known existed was holding out hope. Futile, but I was too exhausted to fight it.

I parked my pickup next to Deacon's. I found him in his office with his mate, Ava.

She was bouncing up and down on the balls of her

feet. A wide smile on her face chased away some of the shadows around my heart. If she was happy, my brother was happy. My state of mind was nothing compared to his and Penn's. My family was my everything. And it would continue to be my everything until I hopefully found a mate of my own.

Sultry doe-brown eyes and that silky brunette hair trailing over my body flashed in my mind.

I had to quit thinking of her before Deacon sensed my arousal. I'd been able to control myself since my teens. He'd know something had changed if I tented my tactical pants in his office.

I dropped into a padded chair across from his desk. "Good news?"

Ava clamped her teeth into her bottom lip, but she couldn't chase away her grin. "It's not *my* good news. And I guess she didn't make it sound like it was *good* news, but I'm really happy. Thrilled for her. I think she'll do just fine."

"So this has nothing to do with your CPA stuff?" Ava planned to open her own business after she became a CPA. She would be a lot of help in the community. We might be dragon shifters, but we still had to do our taxes.

"Nothing to do with accounting. Unless you think that one plus one makes two." A high-pitched squeal emanated from her.

Deacon laughed and tugged Ava onto his lap. "She's pretty excited, if you can't tell."

"I had to play it cool on the phone," she said. "She almost had a panic attack when she told me."

Ava had two best friends. She had to be talking about one of them. I leaned forward, suddenly invested. "What's going on?"

Deacon's gaze jumped to me, my avid focus unlike me. I was observant, but casual. It was easier to read people that way. I reclined in the chair, playing it cool.

Ava jumped up to bounce on her feet. "Avril called. She's pregnant!"

My world closed in, pulsating around my head. Avril was pregnant?

"Who's the dad?" I croaked.

Ava's smile faltered, and she exchanged a glance with Deacon. "Some guy she hooked up with as a rebound," she answered slowly, her blue-green gaze suddenly assessing. "Why?"

I was at the edge of the chair, and I hadn't realized it until I nearly fell off. "When's she due?"

Her eyes narrowed while Deacon's widened.

She continued to study me. "Early next year, like March or February."

I did the math. Abruptly, I stood. "I've gotta take some time off."

Deacon murmured to Ava, but I had put too much distance between us to hear what he said. I charged down the hall to the imposing metal-and-glass doors. Pounding them open, I blew out of city hall. As I was opening the door to my pickup, Deacon caught up with me.

"What's going on?"

I got behind the wheel, but Deacon held the door open and leaned inside, keeping me from being able to slam it in his face. I just really needed to go. Right now.

"Steel. You gotta give me something."

I fired up the engine. "Deacon, there's a good chance that baby is mine."

~

AVRIL

MY BREASTS HURT. I felt perpetually bloated. And tired. So damn tired. As if my rotating shifts didn't mess with my sleep, I hadn't been sleeping well for weeks.

I was a nurse. The changes my body was experiencing shouldn't surprise me. But then if my nursing degree had helped me, I wouldn't have gotten pregnant in the first place. I'd failed at basic protection.

We'd used protection. Steel was as virile as he looked. I was half surprised I didn't get pregnant when I rushed to Silver Lake, thinking Ava needed my help when she'd first met Deacon. Steel had opened the door, and I faced thick, wavy mahogany hair, rich blue eyes, and muscles that I'd only seen on posters and in ads. And my ex was a gym bro.

But Steel's muscles were chiseled and lean. He wasn't built for bulk; he was made for power. And I'd had that power between my legs. A lot.

No wonder the condoms failed.

The pregnancy alone wasn't to blame for my crappy sleep for the last two months. I went to sleep dreaming about him, and when I woke up in the morning, I swore I could still smell his singed-oak scent all over my sheets. I didn't drink bourbon, but his smell made me want to. And every time I woke, disappointment trickled into me when I would stuff my nose into my bedding and only smell my detergent.

I blew out a breath and pictured my longing exhaling with it. Another long shift was over. I had stopped to grab some groceries and was almost home, weaving through a suburb north of Minneapolis. A nice quiet neighborhood that was still big enough to be anonymous in. My home used to be my sanctuary. Now it was only full of memories. Of him.

Steel had checked on me when Venus and Penn had gone to Garnet River to help set up more modern and effective technology for a town as isolated as them. I might've been newly single, but the magic flowing between Venus and Penn was too precious. She had felt bad about ditching me when she'd come out for a visit, but I'd been happy for her. Yet I had still been nursing a heartache from my breakup with Ian.

And Steel had been so... I thought I had gotten lucky with Ian. The ugly duckling landed her Prince Charming. Ian hadn't grown up anywhere near my hometown. He hadn't heard all the rumors about my mom and hadn't witnessed the mean girl club attacking me whenever possible. Ian would be considered hot by many women my age, and he'd certainly seemed both princely and charming. Almost too late, I'd learned he was really arrogant and narcissistic.

I wasn't sure who treated me worse. My ex or the kids who'd made my life miserable in my hometown. The dirt-poor kid of an alcoholic mother who slept with married men didn't fare well when those men were parents of classmates.

I pulled into my garage and shoved off my thoughts of the past before they ruined my whole night. I yawned as I hit the button to shut the garage door. Dinner and bed were in my near future. My twelve-hour shifts at the hospital weren't something I normally looked forward to, but this baby was zapping all my energy. Each hour I worked felt like three.

Even before I had gotten pregnant, every hour I worked had felt like two. I had thought about looking for a new job, but I was stuck now. Benefits, maternity leave, a paycheck I wouldn't be able to find in another field. I had a nursing degree and working in the hospital with differential pay was one of the best wages I could get.

Groaning, I pushed the door open. My stomach twisted. The hunger was always present. Had I lived with Ian so long, getting critiqued about every calorie I put in my mouth, that my appetite rebounded, or was it simply my pregnancy? I got out, and as I turned, I saw a man standing right next to my car.

I yelled and threw a right hook. He caught it in his hand and slid those big talented fingers around my wrist just as I registered it was Steel.

"What the hell are you doing?" I shrieked, my mind and body rioting. I'd gone from terrified to jubilant. Excited swirls danced in my belly like the baby was celebrating Steel's return, and my mind wanted to do the same. I struggled to keep from throwing myself in his arms.

"Ava said you're pregnant." His voice was rough, and I heard the question he didn't utter. Was it his?

I knew when I told Ava that it would get back to Steel. I would've had to tell him eventually, but maybe I had told her first so I could take the coward's way out. "And you're wondering if it's yours?" Was it possible to sound more tired than I felt?

He leaned in until his nose was at my neck and he inhaled. It was weird, dammit, but when he did stuff like that, my belly flipped and tingles spread through my body.

Be strong. I was determined to be a strong single mom. I wasn't my mother. No sinking into a bottle for me just because the man of my dreams walked out. That couldn't happen if there was no man.

Steel had made it clear he would never leave Silver Lake. I had grown up in a town of eight thousand people, and it had been hell. Everyone had known my business. They had known my mother's. And when I lost my virginity to Craig Hefner, the perpetually benched football player who talked a bigger game than he ever got to play, they started a countdown. When would I be a single alcoholic mom like Patti Porter?

Silver Lake had less than a thousand people. The hospital I worked at outside of Minneapolis had more employees than that. People didn't stop spreading rumors after someone turned eighteen. I wasn't going back to that life. No, thank you. My tidy little suburb was ten times bigger than my hometown, and I'd stay here.

He straightened, his warm hand still clasping my wrist. "You haven't been with anyone else."

"Did you smell that?"

His expression didn't change. "I'd like to hear you say it," he said softly.

I owed him that. My father had ditched me and Mom before I got to middle school. I wanted my baby to have a chance to know their dad. How involved Steel would be was up to him.

But I wasn't moving to Silver Lake.

"It's yours." I hadn't been with anyone since Steel. The breakup with Ian had been a couple weeks before

Steel and I had hooked up, and I'd had my monthly in between.

The flashes of sheer panic that had gone through me when I considered that my baby may be my ex's made the relief more acute when I realized it was Steel's. I had nearly collapsed on the bathroom floor.

The dim garage door light cast shadows over his face but couldn't hide the utter possessiveness turning his irises to a color that matched his last name. It fit his first name too and made me remember the sheepish way he grinned when I pointed out how his first and last name went together. Steel looked like he could tear a man apart with his bare hands, but he was warm. Tender. And introspective. Being with him had—

I must enjoy making myself suffer.

I had found out I was pregnant three weeks ago and I had been in a stressful fog since. Steel was all those things, but he'd chosen his town and his job over me. So startlingly similar to my father, it had made me consider keeping the baby secret forever. A silly notion, but selfpreservation didn't always make sense.

Ava was the happiest I'd seen her in Silver Lake with Deacon but hadn't grown up like me. I didn't know the people of Silver Lake, and I would not give them the chance to talk about me or my life's decisions.

Steel hadn't released me. Brushing the fingers of his other hand down my cheek, he kept going, tracing down my neck, over the old T-shirt I had changed into after shedding my scrubs at the hospital, stopping at my belly. Only then, he released my wrist to press both hands against my stomach.

The tender move shoved the wedge of his departure deeper into my heart. "So I take it you're not pissed?"

His gaze jumped to mine, confusion in their silver depths. "Why would I be upset?"

"It's not as if we planned this."

"Some of the best things aren't planned."

This guy. He'd been downright rude when I'd first arrived at Deacon's, ready to throw down to save my best friend. He hadn't gotten much nicer from there. I assumed we tolerated each other's company for those closest to us.

Then he'd stopped to check on me. I'd been having a bad breakup day, crying and feeling sorry for myself. He'd asked what was wrong, and just like that, we'd ended up in bed. And on the floor. In the shower. There was that one time on my kitchen table—

"Well, I guess we have to talk about—" I frowned, his sudden arrival finally sinking in. "I called Ava during my break. You drove all the way here when you found out I was pregnant?"

"Yes."

"Do they know?"

He carefully regarded me, as if he wasn't sure how I'd react. "Yes."

It was inevitable, but damn, I wasn't ready to have my secret out. To be exposed and face the consequences, whatever they were. "And Venus and Penn probably know by now if they know." I should've called Venus, but she was more perceptive than Ava. I worried she'd figure it out, or pester me until I told her.

He dipped his head, and his gaze stroked down my body. I recognized the hot look in his eye. I usually ended up naked.

I laid my hand on his chest—the rock-hard chest I'd had my mouth on several times. "We're done, remember?

I don't think my emotions can handle a casual fling right now."

"What I feel about you isn't casual."

My heart stuttered. I wanted it to be true. I cocked a brow. "So you'll move to Minneapolis?"

His jaw hardened. "I told you I can't."

"We already had our fling. Now we're going to be parents. Let's concentrate on those roles instead of hooking up."

I wasn't sure what I expected. Did I think he was going to beg me to have sex with him? Did I think he was going to relent and say he would move for me and the baby? Did I think I would see more than resignation and determination pass across his face?

"There are things we're going to have to talk about. And you aren't going to like it."

Whatever I had thought he would say, it wasn't that. "I don't get it."

"You don't have to—yet. We still have time. Why don't we go inside." He didn't ask it like a question. More like a command. And there were those traitorous shivers tracing over my skin.

It was hard enough being in my condo without him. But it might be worse for my heart to let him back in. Yet I couldn't bring myself to send him away.

CHAPTER

TWO

S teel

The fatigue lining Avril's face concerned me. She trudged instead of walked, and I stayed behind her, prepared to catch her if she suddenly toppled over.

"Do you work tomorrow?" Concerned or not, my gaze was still drawn to the way her ass cheeks rounded out the thin material of her shorts.

"No, I have the next four days off. Unless they call me to come in."

"You need to tell them no."

She flicked her sandals off inside the condo and went up the stairs. "I don't pass up time and a half."

"Have you eaten yet?" I hadn't stopped for more than gas on my way here. My stomach clenched and twisted, reminding me that breakfast had been shortly after the sun came up, and it was already dark again.

"I managed to get a sandwich eaten on my lunch break."

"It's your lunch break. Why was it hard to eat?"

"It's just the way it is in my field. Sometimes I get a full lunch where I can sit down and everything. Other times, I'm gobbling my food, standing up in front of the break room counter. Some days, I'm lucky to get even water."

"Is it always like that?"

"It goes in phases. There are times when it's really quiet." Her lower lip stuck out like she was troubled. "But lately the quiet shifts seem like they don't happen as much as they used to, but we're always short staffed."

No wonder she was tired. The baby would be demanding a lot of energy her job siphoned. "I'll make us something."

"You don't have to. I was just going to eat another sandwich and go to bed."

My gaze shot straight to her bedroom. To the bed and what we'd done on it had been in my fantasies for two months.

"Alone," she mumbled and wrapped her arms around herself.

She was resisting me, and I didn't know if it was because she truly had no interest in me, or if she was too afraid to take a chance on me, on us. Regardless, she was wiped, and nothing about her said she was into me. I knew her scent, delicate like peonies, and how that scent deepened and grew richer when she was aroused.

There would be no sex tonight.

"Are you hungry?" I asked gently.

The messy bun on top of her head bounced when she nodded.

"Then relax. I'll find something fresh to eat."

In the kitchen, I checked her cupboards and the fridge. They hadn't been this barren when I was here last. Was she really that tired, or was there something else going on?

I was afraid I knew the answer. She was a human growing a shifter baby. And not just any shifter baby, a dragon shifter baby. Every creature on this planet was an energetic being, but dragon shifters were next level. We stored energy for our shifts and for healing.

I would add it to the list of things to talk about. After I figured out how to bring up all the issues tied to this surprise baby.

I found some ground beef in the freezer. I could work with that. "I'll grab some more groceries tomorrow."

"Where are you staying?"

"Here." I tossed the hamburger in the microwave to thaw.

She was about to sink into the couch, but she stopped and stared at me. "Here?"

I wasn't one to force myself on a woman, not physically or emotionally. But I wouldn't be leaving Avril's side. I couldn't win her over in another building, but more importantly, she didn't know how much help she was going to need if she was this exhausted already.

"We have things to talk about, and I can help you with meals and stuff. I'll stay in the room downstairs."

I didn't like the anxiety that rippled over her face. She was scared to have me here. She feared me, but not in the way a woman might typically fear a man. It was like she feared what I represented, and how my presence in her life could change the routine she had grown accustomed to.

And that was why I needed to stay. I needed to figure this human out so I could get her to mate me. Because everything she was resisting was exactly what she was going to have to do.

~

AVRIL

STEEL HAD PRACTICALLY TUCKED me in last night. I'd had the best night's sleep in two months, and I hated to make the connection that it was thanks to the man who had stayed in my guest room. The man who had made homemade hamburgers, using slices of bread like my mom had when I was a kid. And he'd done it without complaint.

I had once made hamburgers and forgot to pick up buns. Ian had thrown a fit. He'd not so jokingly called them trailer trash burgers, and I had laughed with him before shoving the incident out of my mind.

I couldn't *not* think about it last night while eating across from the big man who had a pickup more expensive than the cars Ian and I drove combined. Venus had pointed out his house when I had been in Silver Lake and she, Ava, and I had driven around town. It was an old house, but it looked like it should be on a postcard. Manicured lawn, remodeled exterior. Even the windows were new. Steel Silver had money, and he didn't discuss it. He didn't hold his wealth over my head, and he didn't bat an eye about using plain white bread as a hamburger bun.

Thinking about it made my insides go warm and tingly. And with Steel under my roof, I was fighting a lot of warmth and tingles.

There was a soft tap at the door. I started and yanked the blankets up to my chest. I slept in a tank top and boy-cut shorts. He'd seen me naked, but he hadn't seen me bloated and un-showered. "Yeah?"

He didn't barge in but called through the door. "I was going to head to the store. Want to come with?"

"I have to shower."

"I'll wait."

That simple. No sighs. No huffs that I was intruding on his time. I hadn't planned on going. I was still in bed and wrapping my mind around Steel's presence and what we were going to do for the future. But he'd wait, and I'd rather go than sit around my home and anticipate his return.

"I'll try to be quick." I was also curious. To see a guy like him lumbering through the aisles. Did he just grab bananas, or did he try to pick the perfect shade of yellow? Would he make comments about the items or brands I selected? I used to get all store brand products, but Ian had encouraged me to buy name brands. He insisted. *You're not the poor girl from the trailer park anymore. You should act like it.*

Why was I thinking so much about my ex? The last time Steel and I had spent time together, Ian hadn't crossed my mind. I'd been occupied, my brain delusional from multiple orgasms. But Steel was on the other side of the door, and I couldn't help but compare the two men and realize just how much crap I had put up with when it came to my ex.

"No rush. It's your day off—take your time."

I stared at my closed door. Could a guy really be that handsome and thoughtful? Maybe I was still dreaming.

My stomach cramped and rumbled. Nope. My

monster hunger told me I was wide awake, and I needed to eat before I got nauseated.

Thankfully, my bedroom had a master bath. I did as Steel said. I took my time, as if intentionally testing him.

After my shower, I threw on a pair of jean shorts and an old Cole Swindell concert T-shirt. I braided my still-damp hair into a Dutch braid, something I didn't usually have time for when I was getting ready for work. Satisfied that I didn't look as haggard as I felt, I left the bedroom.

Steel was hunched over the island, scrolling through his phone. A plate was on the counter next to him. Steam rose from it and delicious savory smells caressed my olfactory nerves.

I ignored how much I liked seeing him in my place and focused on the food. "You make omelets too?"

We had barely done more than raid the cupboards when he was here last time. Cooking took too long, and we hadn't been willing to interrupt our sex marathon to prepare an entire meal.

Heat bloomed inside my belly before curling into a tight coil that settled lower than was comfortable. It wasn't uncomfortable, just insistent. After some rest, my worn-out body remembered how blissful this man could make it feel.

"I like to eat, but there's not much for restaurants in Silver Lake. My parents taught me and my brothers to cook. Growing up, we used to take turns."

"I used to cook too, but it was just Hamburger Helper or scrambled eggs."

"Nothing wrong with that."

He watched me as I took the seat beside him, not taking his eyes off me until I cut off a cheesy chunk of the omelet and stuffed it into my mouth. Flavor exploded over my tongue. "Oh my gosh, that's good."

He grunted but went back to his phone.

After I chewed and swallowed, I cut another bite, forcing myself to eat like a lady and not the hungry kid after Mom's payday. "How long are you staying?"

"As long as I need to."

Funny. His brother had said the same thing when he came here looking for Venus after he'd proposed and she ran off. "Are you able to miss work that long?" I sawed the hunk I cut off in half. I was starving, my body demanding the protein, but I would not make a fool of myself.

Without looking, he nudged the plate closer to me. "If you eat, eat. I don't give a shit about manners."

"I do." Normally, I would've lost my appetite, but the empty pit in my stomach wasn't going away. I carefully put a smaller piece of omelet in my mouth.

"To answer your question, yes, I can miss work. This is important. I'll take as much time as I need to, and Deacon understands. As for how you eat in the privacy of your own home, do you really care, or is it something shady that ex of yours said?"

My chewing slowed. "It wasn't just Ian." I put my fingers on my lips. No talking with my mouth full.

Now I had his full attention. "Who?"

"Stupid shit kids say in school."

"Ah, the small-town thing. Why would you get teased about your eating?"

I scraped another bite of omelet away from the rest. It truly was delicious, and I had a powerful urge to put down my fork and bury my face in the plate. But I hoped I wouldn't do that, even with no witnesses. "My mom was depressed before my dad left her, and then she became an alcoholic. We didn't have any family around to help, and my parents weren't exactly doting. I kind of raised myself." A rumble came from his chest. "Are you growling?"

The sound cut off. "I don't like hearing how hard it was for you. That you had two parents, and they failed you."

"Yeah. Maybe it'd have been easier if my classmates were sympathetic, but it felt like I took all the blame for how I was raised. Anyway, after payday, before she spent all her money on booze, we ate like we weren't able to eat the rest of the month."

"And you were teased for it."

"I was on the special lunch program and my school wasn't exactly discreet about it. I was always so hungry by the time lunch came around." I wasn't at school anymore, but I hated to be the unpolished stone around this gleaming marble statue.

He got off the stool and stuffed his phone in his pocket. I thought he would walk away, leaving me to my shame, but he pressed a kiss to my temple. "I'm going to go down to my room, but only because I want you to be comfortable enough to stuff your face and chew with your mouth open. You're going to be hungry, ravenous during this pregnancy. Denying yourself the pleasure of food isn't necessary. Not with me."

And then he was gone, down the stairs, leaving me by myself to stare at the rapidly cooling omelet on my plate.

What he said got to me. I stuffed a chunk that could barely fit into my mouth. My eyes rolled when the warm cheese hit my tongue. Oh, Lord, he had sprinkled chives on the inside. I freaking loved chives.

I cleaned my plate within minutes. My belly was

comfortably full for the first time in what felt like months. Two months, to be exact. It hadn't been the sore boobs and the random nausea that had clued me in to a possible pregnancy. It had been the sharp increase in my appetite. I made a good living, and I fed myself well. But with the gym-fanatic boyfriend, I had watched my food intake. He'd made sure of it. I was used to a certain level of hunger, but this was off the charts. In the grocery store, I was tempted to unload the beef displays into my shopping cart. I liked my meat, but these urges were ridiculous.

It wasn't until I put my plate by the sink that I realized Steel hadn't used the salad-size plates. He'd served the omelet on a larger dinner plate, and it had taken up the entire surface. How many eggs had he used?

I couldn't bring myself to care. Between what he'd said and finally feeling satiated, I wouldn't overthink food for once.

"Tell me when you're ready to head to the store, and we'll take off." Had he hollered from the basement to keep from interrupting my meal? I caught myself smiling.

I smoothed my expression. Ian had put on a good act when I had first met him too, and he turned out to be the conglomeration of all the mean kids in school. Steel was even better looking than him, and he was acting more thoughtful. Plus, he was the father of my baby. When he showed me who he truly was, it would be more devastating than anything else that happened in my life.

THREE

S teel

AVRIL HAD BEEN quiet since we left the condo. I could spend the entire time in the grocery store watching her wander up and down the aisles, studying the way the denim of her shorts molded over her round ass cheeks, and plotting how I would lick over the golden surface of her thick thighs.

Instead, I walked next to her, pointedly pushing a full-size cart and not the little grab-and-go-cart or a carry basket like she had first tried to get. Whenever her gaze lingered on a snack or dessert too long, I snaked it when she wasn't looking and put it in the cart. Did she realize she kept herself in a near-constant state of hunger?

I was a dragon shifter, and my metabolism wasn't like hers, but even humans who were on a permanent diet were full once in a while. It might've started as a money thing, but that was no longer it. She was goddamn gorgeous so it shouldn't be a looks thing, but after her confession this morning, I understood the mental battle. She'd been made to feel ashamed about the way she was. She'd been so powerless, and I had heard enough about her ex to know that he likely used it as a method of control.

She'd need time to heal, but she was pregnant with a dragon shifter baby. She needed to eat or that baby would consume her.

When she asked how long I was staying, I meant it when I said as long as I needed to, but I couldn't explain that I knew how long I would need to. At the minimum, I would stay until she gave birth. I would ensure she received the care and nutrition she needed, but the question she really needed to ask was how long *she* was going to stay. Because that was a tough topic I would have to broach later.

"You need to put that back." She was eyeing the Double Stuf Oreos I had tossed in the cart. "I have ice cream at home—I don't need more goodies."

"Do you like Double Stuf Oreos?"

She looked at me like I asked her if she liked puppies. "Of course. Doesn't everyone?"

"Then why not get them?"

"Because I'll eat that package."

"You're pregnant, Avril. If you feel like eating, you need to eat."

She rolled her eyes and studied a box of fiber bars. "I'm sure my OB would disagree with you."

I was sure her OB hadn't dealt with this type of pregnancy. "The babies in my family demand a lot of energy to grow. When you're hungry, it's because the baby inside of you is telling you it needs fuel."

"That's not quite how it works, Steel."

She was a nurse. She would think she knew more about this than me, and when it came to human babies, yes, she did. But she wasn't carrying a human child, and I couldn't exactly come out and tell her in the snack aisle of the grocery store. "If you get those fiber bars, I'm adding another package of Oreos."

She scowled, but interest flared in her eyes. She wanted to object to a second package of Oreos, but she couldn't. She bypassed the fiber bars. "Just quit throwing junk food into the cart."

I'd stop. For now. "You need more eggs."

Without arguing, she meandered to the meat section. While she was choosing a package of boneless, skinless chicken breasts, I dumped in a few roasts, several pack-ages of sirloin and ribeye steaks, and picked a couple packages of stew meat.

She turned with the Styrofoam tray of chicken in her hand. Her eyes widened when she saw my selections. "Carnivore much?"

"We need a lot of protein. It's genetic. Therefore, you're going to want a lot of protein."

"Whatever," she muttered and wandered to the dairy case. I followed, grabbing a couple of stuffed pork chops as I went.

She was bending over a display of yogurt when the dude bro I had met the first time I was at her place rounded the corner with a petite woman at his side.

"Jesus. Avril?"

I stopped the cart next to Avril and wished one of the

abilities being a dragon shifter gave me was laser vision. This asshole would be dust.

Avril sighed before she straightened. "Hi, Ian," she said in a dead tone.

Satisfaction that she wasn't happy to see him, while at the same time not being devastated, tamped down the rage that was building toward this human. He had hurt her—intentionally and unintentionally. I wouldn't allow him to do it again.

"What are you—" His gaze landed on me and recognition flared. A red flush crept up his neck and into his cheeks. He'd been humiliated by Venus the last time he had seen me. He draped an arm over the tiny woman.

He seemed like a gym guy. I had nothing against gyms or workout facilities, but I had everything against men like him who trolled those spaces for vulnerable women. Ian wasn't a man who looked for just any woman in the workout space. He was the type who spotted those punishing themselves because of past or present trauma. I hoped his new girlfriend caught on quickly and got away. But her youthful, open expression said she was probably still in college or had just graduated. Ian might be getting older, but the women he went after would always be the same age.

"This is my new girlfriend, SaRaye."

"Nice to meet you, SaRaye." Warmth infused Avril's voice.

"Who's he?" Ian asked in a hard tone. He might've broken up with Avril, but he didn't like seeing her with anyone else.

Avril looked from me to Ian. She might've had a good night's sleep and a couple of solid meals, but fatigue simmered in her eyes. I couldn't tell if she was physically tired, or emotionally sick of Ian's bullshit. I had my answer soon enough. "This is Steel, my baby's dad."

Ian's eyes bugged open, and I fought a smile. I'd rather be called her boyfriend, or her fiancé, but she acknowledged me in public. I'd take that for now.

"You're pregnant?" Disbelief and disgust mixed in Ian's expression as he looked her up and down. "That explains it."

I ditched the shopping cart and stood between Avril and Ian. "You make one more comment about her looks, her size, or anything else that isn't genuinely complimentary, I will crush you. I will crush your body, I will crush your soul, I will crush your hopes and your dreams. Do you understand me?"

Ian was average height for a human man, and he had a stocky, muscular body, all the way down to his narrow calves. I was taller and bigger, and the look in my eye likely promised I would follow through on everything I said.

He stepped back. His new girlfriend edged to the side. Her movement caught my attention.

I adopted a compassionate expression when I faced her. "Some helpful advice you might not want, but you probably need. Everything this man says is selfish. His actions and his words are meant for him, not for you, and if that means he has to hurt you in order to make himself feel better or more important, then he will. You're better leaving sooner than later."

Hostility was building in Ian's gaze until I turned my attention back to him and it morphed into fear.

"Now, I want you to apologize to my woman. And then I want you to make sure you never forget what I said."

Ian didn't look at Avril as he mumbled his apology and dragged SaRaye away.

Because I needed to do something with the aggression riding on a tidal wave in my veins, I grabbed an armload of yogurt and dumped it into the cart.

After watching me, Avril said nothing until I met her gaze. "I'm not sure if I should be really pissed at you, or thanking you, but I'm pretty sure I should feel guilty about how much I enjoyed what you did."

"Never feel guilty around me. What else is on your list?"

She bit back a smile. "Milk."

"As long as you don't complain when I grab two gallons of chocolate milk, lead the way."

~

AVRIL

WE WERE home after the shopping trip. Steel had insisted on carrying all the groceries in and putting them away, strongly urging me to take a nap. I only obliged to put some space between us. And because I was tired. Again.

My heart still pounded after the way he'd talked to Ian. I had worried they would start a fight in the store, and I anticipated it. After what Venus had done when she was here, Ian wouldn't be fooled again. Selfishly, I had wanted to see Steel in action. I knew he could move his body in ways most other men couldn't—definitely not Ian.

I hadn't experienced one spike of jealousy when Ian introduced SaRaye. I used to go to the same gym he went to. That was where we met. I knew a lot of the people who worked out there, the regulars. There were the middle-aged men and women who were only interested in fitness. Then there was the younger crowd who were also only interested in fitness but were seeking like-minded people. And finally there was the meat market. Toward the end of our relationship, my paranoia that Ian was using the gym more like a meat market had been well founded.

It was possible he even cheated on me with SaRaye. And I... didn't care.

Two months ago, I would've been devastated. Even after Venus's visit when she asked me if I was better off without him, and I realized I was, I would've still gotten home and crumpled in a ball, sobbing my eyes out. I would've spent the rest of the day comparing myself to petite SaRaye. Her muscles were more defined, her butt had the definition I'd been trying to achieve with years of squats and reverse lunges, and she had those dainty ankles that I admired. I come from a long line of cankles. Ian would constantly remind me to do my calf raises.

And Steel had threatened him.

I had loved it.

I didn't know what to do with the man in my condo. I wanted him so badly, but geography was keeping us apart. I couldn't afford to get hurt again. I wanted him in the baby's life; I was going to be alone enough as it was. But I had to protect my heart.

There was a knock at the door. "Avril?"

I didn't respond. Maybe he would think I was still sleeping.

"I know you're awake. Are you hungry?"

Dammit, I was hungry. I was nearly as hungry as I

had been this morning. "How did you know I was awake?"

I expected him to say he heard me tossing and turning, which I hadn't been. But he didn't speak for a moment. "It's part of something we'll talk about later."

"Your family has a condition with their hearing?"

I heard a soft chuckle through the door. "Yeah, something like that."

I sat up and crossed my legs, pulling the covers up to my waist. I was wearing the same shirt I had on this morning, but had changed into elastic workout shorts. All the pants and shorts in my wardrobe that had buttons and zippers wouldn't be useful for very much longer. I thought most women could wear their regular clothes through the first trimester, but eating was becoming my superpower, so I guess I'd have to upgrade my wardrobe sooner.

"What are these family conditions you're talking about?" Before I had fallen asleep, I distracted myself from the way Steel's aggression excited me by pondering his family's medical history. He and his brothers were tall, but they weren't unusually tall. They were fit and muscular, but again, they could blend into a crowd. The thing that made them stand out was their looks, but they weren't the only handsome men on the planet. Steel may be the sexiest man in the world, but he'd given me so many orgasms I wasn't exactly objective.

"Can I come in?"

Absolutely not. Steel in my bedroom? That was how I had gotten into this mess.

I said "yes" before my lips could form the word no.

He strode in like he owned the place. I couldn't summon the ability to tell him to stop before he reached the bed, but he only perched on the end, as if he sensed I couldn't handle him being too close. I had to be strong. I needed to protect my heart, but I wasn't superhuman. If the distance was keeping us from being together, then it would help me resist him.

"We need to talk."

The gravity in his voice made me sit straighter. "What's wrong?"

Was this where he asked me to leave him out of the baby's life? Or worse, to terminate the pregnancy so he could be completely free of me? As soon as I realized I was expecting, I became determined to do everything I could for this kid. I'd already bonded.

"There's no easy way to tell you this. You're not going to believe me. And when you do believe me, you're going to hate me. Hopefully, only for a little while."

"Oh my god, you're married." Wouldn't Ava have said something? Steel didn't act taken.

"No, but that would be easier for you to deal with than this."

What the hell did that mean? Anxiety replaced some of the hunger in my stomach.

He propped his arms on his thick thighs and rubbed his hands together as he pensively stared at the floor. "Your hunger feels out of control because the baby you're growing requires a lot of energy and protein. Because it's not human."

I barked out a laugh. Of all the worst-case scenarios I had run through my head, an aluminum-foil-hat-wearing Steel wasn't one of them. "Aliens?"

"Dragon shifter."

A nervous chuckle. His expression was so serious my smile died. "Come on, Steel." Just like he hadn't acted taken, he didn't act like he was out of touch with reality. Dragons? Shifters?

"I'll explain it before I demonstrate it, but I can't fully show you in here. Your place is too small, and I can't risk being spotted through your mini blinds."

He would show me what? A dragon? Someone was doing too much reading of *Games of Thrones*. Only they didn't shift. So what was going through his mind? "I'll bite. Tell me the story."

"My kind existed before humans took over the earth. We traded in our immortality to blend among the humans, to become more human. The writing was on the wall. Humans were going to take over, and after centuries of war over the decision, there was no other choice. We have the average lifespan of a human. We can reproduce like a human, where before there could be centuries between births. We live in our human form, but can shift to a dragon. But since we're still shifters, we must live among our clans. It's why I can't leave Silver Lake."

His solemn tone and complete belief in what he was saying stunned me. "You can't leave Silver Lake because you're a dragon shifter?"

"Yes, dragon shifters rule over the other shifters."

A disbelieving sound ripped out of my throat. "Other shifters? Like what?"

In all seriousness, he said, "Mountain lions, bears, wolves."

I stared at him. His delusion was bone deep. And this was the father of my baby. I wanted him in our kid's life, but what if... what if he was delusional? What if he was a danger to our child and himself? My nausea had nothing to do with morning sickness.

"The reason you're going to hate me, Avril, is because

you're pregnant with a dragon shifter baby. That means the baby cannot be raised in human society. And because I've told you about us, because you *have* to know, you will need to become my mate."

More disbelieving snorts resonated from my throat until I wasn't sure I could form coherent words. "I'm sorry, what? You're telling me you're going to try to take my baby?"

"I won't try, Avril. It's imperative our baby is raised among its kind. Our children go to shifter schools in the towns our clans have formed. We can't risk putting them in a human classroom where they might get upset and shift. Little dragons running through a playground wouldn't be good for my people."

"That's ridiculous." The other part of what he said was equally ludicrous. "And what's this mating thing?"

"Like a marriage. Only we're bonded by more than vows."

I snorted again. "We'd have to marry. Isn't that archaic?"

"It's necessary to protect our people."

"How romantic." Sarcasm dripped from my voice.

His gaze stroked over my face, making me acknowledge my disappointment. And for what? A guy I had turned down who just declared he had to marry me —*mate* me—because he had to. Be still my heart.

And it was absurd that I was even upset. I turned him down. I didn't want this.

"I've been drawn to you since I met you. I've wanted you since I opened the door at Deacon's place. But you were taken. I tried to stay away, Avril. I did. I didn't want to put you in this situation. But it's against our laws for a human to know about us and not be mated to one of our kind."

Despite the bizarre story he was telling, my mind stuck on his confession that he wanted me. Since he first saw me. My traitorous heart swooned while my brain told it to settle the hell down. This man was dangerous.

Before now, I thought he was dangerous to my heart. But I didn't know him. I didn't even know his middle name. I knew who his brothers were, who his sister-in-law was, and where he lived. Other than that, I knew very little about this man. And my baby and my life were his?

I swayed backward until my back hit the headboard. My breathing grew more rapid and my gaze darted around the room.

"I'm not going to hurt you, Avril," he said softly. "Not physically, but I know that uprooting your life and moving you to Silver Lake is going to emotionally hurt you, and for that, I'm sorry."

"I don't believe you. I don't believe a thing you're saying."

He let out a long, heavy breath and looked away. When he brought his gaze back to me, his eyes were a more brilliant blue than before. His cheekbones grew more prominent along with his entire body, until the seams of his shirt and pants strained against his body.

I gasped, and in a second he was back to being himself.

"I'm imagining this."

He shook his head, his gaze sympathetic. "No, you didn't." He lifted his chin to where my phone rested on my nightstand. "Call Ava and ask her."

"You think Ava's going to vet your story?"

"Ava didn't marry my brother. She mated him. I'll let her explain the situation. It's not my story to tell. But talk to her. Talk to her before you do anything." His tone bordered on a warning, like he knew I was pondering how fast I could call for help before he overpowered me. I should be plotting to do that, but it hadn't occurred to me.

"Fine."

He dipped his head. "I'll give you some privacy."

I dialed Ava and willed her to answer just as much as I hoped she was too busy to.

Her sunny voice came through the line. "Hey, I've been thinking about you."

"Why? Because you know I'm pregnant with a dragon shifter baby and you didn't tell me?" My laugh lacked humor.

She met my comment with silence.

"Oh, god, Ava. You don't believe in all this, do you?"

"It's true, Avril. It's all true."

"So you've actually seen Deacon turn into a dragon? And Steel?"

"I haven't seen Steel shift, but yes, I've seen Deacon turn into a dragon. When you get to know Steel, it'll all make sense. But they do shift, and they're good guys."

Denial ran rampant through me. What were the odds both Steel and my childhood best friend shared the same alternate reality? "No. No, it can't be true. This is ridiculous. Because if it's true, he said that my baby can't be raised in my home. He said that I would have to move. He said I would have to mate him."

"It's for the safety of their people. I'm so sorry," Ava whispered.

My denial was growing elusive. I would not believe his story. "No, dammit. You're all lying."

"I know how you feel, I really do. Deacon tied me to him without me knowing what was involved, like Steel did to you. I know the pregnancy was accidental, and he had to tell you, but it still feels unfair because it is."

"I'm not moving back to a tiny town with a man I can't trust."

"Why can't you trust Steel?"

"Because I can't." I waited for a thousand reasons to pop into my head, but none did. I knew they were there. They'd reveal themselves soon enough. That was how it worked with men. "I worked hard for this life. I worked hard to get away from that town. I'm not going to a place one-eighth its size. I'm not going back to being the outsider no one gives a damn about."

Although wasn't that what Ava was going through? And yet every time I talked to her since she had met Deacon, she was deliriously happy.

How bad could Silver Lake be?

No. I wasn't buying it. Ava was no me. She hadn't grown up like me. Her parents had loved and were dedicated to each other, and to her. "Look, I'll talk to you later."

"All right, I get it. But give yourself time. If nothing else, you need to give yourself time to think about this."

"According to Steel, I have nothing to think about. He controls me. I thought the relationship I just got out of was controlling, but this is a stratospheric level I didn't know existed."

"It's not like that. It won't be like that. Just give it time, Avril. Please. You've known me your entire life. Please believe me and give yourself time."

Ava had been my only friend when I had nothing and no one. "Fine."

I hung up before she could say anything. I was too frustrated, too disconcerted, to keep arguing, to keep trying to poke holes in a story that my best friend, the person I would believe if she told me the earth was flat and the moon was made of cheese, believed.

I whipped the blankets off and stomped to the living room.

Steel was hunched over the island, his hands folded together and his head hanging down, like he was waiting for the executioner to call his name.

"I can't get over the hurdle of believing any of this. So if you really want me to buy that you're a dragon shifter, and I've got not-a-human in my belly, then you're going to have to go full"—I waved my hand like I was wielding a magic wand—"dragon."

The next move was his.

CHAPTER
FOUR

S teel

I HAD DRIVEN this area enough times two months ago that it was all too familiar. I didn't think I would be back in the Garnet River area anytime soon, and I would've never guessed it was to bring Avril out and prove to her I was a dragon shifter.

She peered out the window at the passing trees. "Garnet River is a dragon shifter colony?"

"We say clan, but yes."

She had been on the quiet but hostile side. I couldn't blame her. It was one thing to find out that humans weren't alone on this earth, and another to learn that she would have to change her entire life because she had slept with me.

"So the work Penn and Venus said they were doing for Deacon out here was what?"

"Again, that's not my story to tell. Venus will be happy to fill you in now that you know about us, but before we turn thirty-five, we're supposed to have a mate. We're still part beast, and our aggression can get out of control. A mate helps stabilize us and is also a built-in welfare check. One of the reasons we live around our own kind is so we can keep an eye on each other."

"So the reason Venus had to get married to Penn, or what you call mated, is because she was turning thirty-five?"

Her tone still claimed that everything I said was bull-shit. "Like me, Venus is from a ruling family. We set the example. If we aren't mated by our thirty-fifth birthday, then we are executed. Venus almost chose death over Penn."

"She wouldn't."

"She's that stubborn, and you know it."

"She'd actually be killed for staying single?"

"Yes. We get dangerous. That hiking accident story she told you when Penn and I got hurt?"

Avril flicked her gaze to me, confusion on her face. "Where you got banged up? That was a lie?"

"Deacon asked us to check on a feral shifter—that's what we call a shifter who hasn't mated and is slowly losing their mind to their aggression. While we were checking out an anonymous tip that Garnet River's ruler hadn't done her job when it came to a feral shifter, we were attacked. Technically, there was more going on, but the feral shifter also had a sibling going feral. We were shot, and they were going to eat us."

She twisted in her seat. "What? That's absurd."

She'd have an easier time believing it when she saw

my dragon, and my large teeth, my talons, and my spiny ridges. "It's not. It's our nature and we have to be very careful with our dragons. So if Venus wanted to make the decision to be single, she was also deciding to endure the punishment. Which is death."

"Who would've killed her? What happened to the feral shifters?" It was a good sign she was invested in the story, but I wasn't sure how much she actually believed.

"The clan ruler is supposed to carry out the punishment, but they can assign the task to someone else like Deacon did with us because Penn and I were here already and Garnet River's ruler wasn't doing it. But shifters aren't designed to withstand bullet wounds, so Venus saved our ass and terminated the ferals."

When I glanced over, her forehead was still furrowed. "The ruler is the…"

"Mayor. They're officially the mayor of the town on the books."

Morbid disbelief rang in her tone. "So Venus's brother would've had to kill her?"

I left my answer at a nod.

She slumped back in her seat. "That's messed up. But back to Garnet River—you're still alive. And you don't have any bullet wound scars." Color flooded her face.

She'd know. She'd seen and tasted almost every inch of my body. "We heal quickly, and Venus saved us before the wound became too dire to recover from."

"What about the rest of the time? When Venus and Penn went out there to stay?"

"The ruler of Garnet River was young and inexperienced, and she was being targeted by a shifter family who wanted power for their own selfish reasons. So Venus and

Penn offered to help train Brighton Garnet, and then the family that was causing issues in the clan attacked her. My brothers and I, and her brothers, had to save her."

She stared at me for several moments, disbelief continuing to churn in her eyes. "And Ava was in on all this?"

"I know you want to be angry with her, but the penalty for spilling our secrets is death, so..."

"How compassionate." Her sarcasm was strong enough to smother her natural peony scent. "You get a death penalty and you get a death penalty." She made a disgusted sound in her throat.

"The safety of our kind is critical, Avril. We could be studied. We could be left alone, but if our rules aren't adhered to, then the aggression becomes unleashed. The shifter trait is dominant. Our baby will be a shifter. It's the same for all kinds of shifters. If we start roaming freely and the world embraces us?" I shook my head. My position in the clan meant I saw our kind when we were at our worst. "Shifter genes can't be allowed to go unchecked. It'll kill more people than the rules you hate."

Her jaw went tight, and she stared out the window. She still didn't like it, but maybe she understood a little better.

"We have some tools to help keep humans safe from our laws. Ruling families have special abilities. Some ruling shifters can heal, like if a human gets injured by a shifter. A shifter wasn't involved, but Deacon used his ability and saved Ava's father. And I can wipe a memory here and there, in case a human sees or hears something they shouldn't. We think Penn's brains are to help us adapt. The better we can blend with humans and understand the need for our laws, the less of the death penalty we have to use."

"Wait—what happened to Ava's dad?"

"He was dying, Avril." I made my tone as grave as the situation had been. "He would've been dead if Deacon hadn't been there. No ambulance would've gotten to him in time."

Her face lightened a few shades. "Have you wiped people's memories?"

"Yes, a few. We settled in rural areas where there are a lot of trees and concealment, but occasionally a human witnesses a shift. Someone like me can step in and wipe out those few moments."

"When have you used it?"

My hand tightened on the steering wheel. "Five years ago, a dad and his daughter were fishing at Silver Lake. They didn't realize it was private property and they saw one of the townsfolk shift."

"They would've had to die."

I took my eyes off the road to look at her. She had to see how seriously we took our rules, and how hard they could be to live by. "Deacon and I would've had to kill them. A father and his daughter, Avril. But I was able to remove the entire memory of Silver Lake, and we drove them to Wildrose. Told the clinic we found them disoriented and confused. They got counseled on the importance of hydration while hiking and also how to note private property signs."

"Would you have done it?"

The word "yes" hovered on my lips. There was a shitty aspect to my job, to my role in my clan, but could I have killed them—or let Deacon? Could Deacon have done it? "I don't know, but those scenarios are why I do my job. They're why Venus was willing to die, and I'm willing to uproot your life to bring you to Silver Lake. We'll set the example that'll keep others from getting innocents hurt."

I wished she'd tell me what she was thinking. She contemplated her intertwined hands in her lap. She swallowed hard. "It's funny that out of everything you said, I find that the most believable."

I wanted to touch her, to stroke her face and tell her it'd be all right. But we'd driven all the way to Garnet River, in the middle of nowhere, so she could see the undeniable truth. I put the pickup in gear and ambled down the road to a turnoff for a familiar, now vacant, shop.

This was where Venus had been held after she was captured by the family who was after Brighton. The family had been dealt with, all except one and he was Brighton's problem.

I parked in front of the building. "No one will see us here." She nodded, but the sour tint to her floral smell betrayed her anxiety. "It'll be okay."

She gave me a "seriously?" look. Right. I was going to turn into a dragon in front of her eyes and it'd confirm all the bad news I had laid on her.

I got out and walked farther down the road where I wouldn't be impeded by trees. Avril finally climbed out of the pickup. She stayed by the open door with her arms crossed.

I took off my shirt and tossed it on the ground. My boots and jeans were next.

"Why are you undressing?" Her question rang with alarm.

"I don't want to shred my clothing."

She crossed her arms and lifted her chin, but didn't look away. I let the shift take over, energy flowing through my body as it expanded. My bones elongated and my skin transitioned to scales. It wasn't like dragons could look into mirrors, but I shifted enough with my brothers to know what I looked like. A silver sheen over my green scales, blue eyes that were still mine, and a long spiked tail.

I kept my gaze on her, prepared to shift back and catch her if she tried to use the pickup to escape me. If she took off on foot, I'd let her run through the trees for a while as long as she wasn't so frantic she hurt herself.

I waited, holding my breath.

She stared at me for so long, and she was so still, I tried to say her name, momentarily forgetting that I was a damn dragon. Her eyes widened when my mouth gaped open. I snapped it shut and hung my head, hoping to convey my apology for scaring her.

She hugged herself tighter, but she didn't take her gaze off me. Nor did she run, or cry, or scream. She was as still as a statue. Until her face crumpled, and she dropped to her knees, burying her head in her hands. Then the sobs started.

~

AVRIL

"THIS CAN'T BE HAPPENING," I sobbed. It'd been a few minutes since he'd changed. Right in front of my damn eyes.

He held me, thankfully as a man, stroking my shoulders and rubbing my back. My distress was almost enough to make me forget he was naked.

I drew in a shuddering breath. "You can't be that thing, and I can't be pregnant with your baby, and I can't lose everything."

"I don't want to take anything from you, Avril," he murmured into my hair. "I want to give you everything, but the fact is, I can't do it here."

I cried harder. Fierce protectiveness surged through me. This baby could change into—a *dragon*. I wouldn't let anyone turn it into a science project. My baby would not be studied.

If anything, it would be as magnificent as its father. Steel was nothing like CGI dragons, like nothing Hollywood could depict. The silver sheen that gleamed over his body matched his last name. That probably wasn't a coincidence, but what did I know? A dragon that moved, that reflected sunlight, that blended with the land like it belonged, not like it was fake.

I'd slept with a man who wasn't a man and now I had to trade the life I worked so hard for. "What am I going to do?"

"We'll make it work."

Make it work. Wasn't that what a girl always wanted to hear?

Your dad left us, but we'll make it work.

My mom can't give you a ride because of your mom. Hope you can make something else work.

We don't have any money until payday. Make what groceries we already have work.

I always made it work and dammit, I was tired. Now I was alone, pregnant with a dragon shifter's baby. I didn't want to have to make motherhood work. After seeing what I was ready to settle for with Ian, I had been determined not to make another relationship "work." And look how that turned out.

I pushed away from him and rose on shaky legs. "You need to get dressed."

"Something's bothering you."

"You think?" I tried to pin him with a glare, but I couldn't hold it. He was gloriously nude. Wide chest kissed by the sun. Abs I had traced with my fingers and tongue. And when my gaze landed on his cock, it twitched.

I jerked my attention off of him.

"Aside from all the other stuff," he said, not at all moving to get dressed, "what did I say that upset you?"

He knew my issues with quitting my job and moving to Silver Lake. The extra layer of complication a dragon shifter baby adds. I might as well tell him the rest. "A girl doesn't grow up dreaming she'll hear the man she's going to spend her life with say he'll 'make it work.'" I turned to get into the pickup, then spun to face him again, keeping my gaze glued to his gray-blue eyes and not the rest of his naked body. "Growing up, seeing my mom put everything in her relationship to completely lose herself when my dad left made an impression. It said I shouldn't settle for a man who doesn't make me a priority—and I was almost fooled by Ian."

"And you think you're nothing but a default?"

I gave him a tight, humorless smile. "But we'll make it work, right?"

I got in the passenger seat and stared out the windshield. Crossing my arms to signal that I was done with today's conversation about babies and shifters and relationships, I tried to ignore Steel, as if that was possible.

A couple of minutes later, he got behind the wheel, dressed back in his blue jeans and white T-shirt. He didn't immediately start the pickup. He sat like me and looked out the windshield.

"I wish we could do this differently," he said, his voice soft, but serious. "My job and my family come first. They always have, and they always will. Because I was born a Silver. But, Avril, that doesn't mean you're any less important to me. You and the baby will be my family too. You're not a default. I wanted to be with you, but you turned me down."

"For the reasons you just mentioned." His people came first. He couldn't leave Silver Lake. "And we've circled right back. Just a ring of issues between us that make me dizzy."

I brushed my gaze over his profile. He was a good guy. Any other girl would be so damn lucky to have him. Some other girl who didn't have my past. Who wasn't terrified to leave the anonymity of the big city. Some other girl who didn't desperately want to be someone's everything so maybe she could trust in his love.

I didn't think he loved me. When he'd asked me to go with him two months ago, he might've been infatuated. It was hard to tell. He came off as constantly irritated. But when it came to sex, he was focused and gave a hundred and ten percent. I only knew him a little better since he appeared in my garage. He was passionate. But he wasn't passionate about me. Not me, *specifically*.

My decision was instant, but once made, I was set. "I'm staying in Minnesota until the baby's born."

"Avril—"

"Nonnegotiable. I'm going to work and save up as much money as I can. I'm not going to be dependent on you in a town full of strangers. When I move, I'll do what I have to do to preserve my life, and I want you in the baby's life, but I'm not going to be just another job for you."

His dark brows dropped. "You aren't my job."

"You have to raise your shifter baby from the woman you knocked up in another state, and you have to be with me because you had to tell me what you were. If that isn't what you explained to me before you shifted, I don't know what is."

"I can't stay here until the baby's born. You have to come to Silver Lake."

I crossed my arms so hard my boobs ached even worse than before. "Is there a law that says a shifter baby has to gestate in Silver Lake?"

A muscle jumped in the corner of his jaw. "No."

"Does one of your laws state that I have to mate you immediately after you told me about you, or is my word enough?"

"You can't go making promises and giving your word to shifters. Breaking it could cost your life."

"Like Ava and Deacon?"

His nod was grim. He hadn't approved of what his brother had done, and I softened even more toward him against my will. This guy would be perfect if he was human and was actually in love with me.

"So there's nothing against me living in my condo in Minnesota until the baby is born?"

The muscles on each side of his jaw ticked. "Avril—"

"Look, Steel. I'm sure you're used to getting your way,

but this is my life. Don't you think waiting six months to destroy it is the least you could do?"

My words were harsh, and my regret was instant. Anguish filled his eyes, softening me from the inside out. "I don't want to destroy your life, but my job is protecting my people. I can't do that if my people are in different places."

The struggle to be resolute was shocking. I wanted to hug the stress from his eyes. This was hard on both of us, but I needed time to process everything. Time to figure out how I could keep my identity when I'd be relegated to *his* mate and the mother of *his* child. I had to figure out how to keep from being my mom. "Six more months."

Because if I went now—dragon shifter or not—he could melt me into a puddle and spread me around with a greasy rake and I wouldn't complain. I'd seen the threat of Steel Silver to my sanity when we first slept together. And when he'd asked me to go with him to Silver Lake, I had nearly laughed as I rejected him.

Perhaps I was learning the real reason I stayed with Ian and tolerated his toxic attitude. I could keep my walls up. Ian couldn't sweep me under his magnetism.

Steel could obliterate my guards, but he was too considerate to do that. I could safely reject him and I couldn't say that about many men.

"Can I stay with you a little longer?" he asked, proving that I could easily succumb to him. His sincere tone. The way he looked at me like he was really concerned about me. And he was because that was the kind of guy he was. He'd take care of me until I didn't know how to care for myself. And I'd seen the outcome of that. "Then I can travel back and forth until the due date."

I shouldn't hate the idea of him leaving so much that hearing him ask to stay with me longer sends a teasing thrill through my body. "Yeah, I guess it's a good idea. There'll be appointments and stuff."

He nodded and fired up the engine. The trip back home was silent.

CHAPTER
FIVE

S teel

I THOUGHT the whole dragon shifter thing would be the biggest hurdle between me and Avril. But the distance between us could just as well put us in separate solar systems. I tried to understand, but it was like fighting a phantom in the dark with my eyes closed.

She'd been hurt before I came along and I was suffering the consequences. All I could do was be there for her and try to keep her resentment of me to a minimum.

She was at work and I was sitting at the island memorizing the lines in the full granite pattern while I thought about what I could do for her. Our chemistry was off the charts. How could it be so hard between us?

I didn't want to let down the woman who would become my mate. I didn't want her to have a harder time accepting the human side of me than the dragon side. I spent my life watching Deacon's back and protecting Silver Lake. I watched over my little brother, and I broadened the zones I patrolled to watch over my people.

But I couldn't be the guy Avril needed.

Deacon's name flashed across my phone as it buzzed against the countertop. I tapped it and put the speaker on.

"How did it go?"

I didn't need to ask him how he knew. I was sure that as soon as Ava got off the phone with Avril, she told Deacon what was going on. Technically, it was my job to inform Deacon that a human who was not yet mated to a shifter knew about us. I had been preoccupied.

"It went as expected."

"She lost her mind?"

I was tempted to leave Deacon with his assumptions, but I needed to say it. Maybe getting the words out would keep them from swirling in my mind, creating chaos out of my thoughts. "She lost her shit, yeah, but not for the reason you think."

"I thought you shifted in front of her? Brighton said you notified her you were taking Avril there."

"I shifted. She saw it all. But that wasn't why she had a breakdown."

"Because of you?" The disbelief in Deacon's voice made me feel a tiny bit better.

"She doesn't want to leave the city. She doesn't want to be in Silver Lake. She told me a little about what it was like growing up, why she despises small towns, and she hates that she would feel like just another job to me."

"And how do you feel?"

I scowled at the phone. I felt like a giant pile of crap. "What do you mean?"

"I mean, how do you feel about the situation? You're telling me about what Avril thinks, but what do you think about Avril and the baby?"

"I don't know her that well." But I had craved her since I first saw her, and the urges had grown worse since we were together.

"Do you like her?"

"I'm not a five-year-old on a playground, Deacon."

"Then answer the question."

I let out a gusty sigh. "I want her, but she turned me down once already. I was ready to commit. She was the one. And she shot me down. She didn't want to move to a place that has everyone I care about and that I've dedicated my life to. Pretty hard to come back from that."

"How do you feel about the baby?"

"She's not eating enough. Between the way she grew up and that ex of hers, she's been programmed to eat less than she needs. I'm afraid that if I'm not around, she won't eat enough protein and she'll get sick. It'll harm her, and harm the baby." Speaking of which, I needed to plan what I would make for breakfast. She worked all night and would be home in the morning. I didn't want her to collapse into bed without nourishment.

"Those are the logistics of the baby, Steel. How do you *feel?*"

I sank my head into my hand, dragging my fingers through my hair. I was thirty-three, and for the last ten years, I had dreamed of finding a mate and starting a family. Silver Lake was small, and unlike my brothers, I didn't go away for college. I had graduated and went right to patrolling Silver Lake and the surrounding area. I spent a lot of time alone, and when I went out, the females I found came to my bed easy enough. But like Avril, they had wanted more, and the middle Silver brother with the mundane job wasn't it.

"I haven't thought about it much, honestly." And that was the truth. I had been so worried about what to tell Avril, when, and how I would do it, I hadn't thought about what came after. A rounded belly with my young. Feeling my baby kick through my mate's skin. Sleepless nights and diapers. Longing tugged heavy on my heart until I was afraid I would flip inside out. "I want to be happy, Deacon." My words came out strangled. Emotions clogged my throat and I couldn't continue.

"But you're afraid."

"I never thought I would have to worry about my mate hating me."

"She doesn't hate you or you wouldn't be in her place." He said it so confidently, I almost believed him. "You like her, right?"

I liked how she looked. Curves for miles. Flesh and muscle I could sink my fingers and teeth into. A throaty laugh and then an introspective gaze. And the sex—phenomenal. If I could choose one thing to do for the rest of my life, it would be indulging in her body every chance I had.

But what had gotten to me about her those two weeks we were together were the times we weren't doing it. The comfortable moments between us when she would flip through channels and we'd comment on shows. She'd read a book on her side of the bed while I scanned through my phone, catching up on emails and looking up legal courses that would help me in my line of work.

We might not have a lot in common, but I was comfortable around her. And that was what had been missing with everyone else. A sense of acceptance. I didn't have to live up to anyone's expectations, and I didn't have to worry about not being my brothers. I was just Steel around Avril. Until it came to where we'd live. Then I couldn't reach the lowest rung of her expectations.

"I like her a lot," I admitted. "I want us to be a happy family. But without what she thinks are the basics, I don't know what to do."

Deacon was quiet for a few moments. "You guys haven't known each other long, but there's obviously a connection. You've acted different around her since day one. She's special to you, and you're going to have to show her. You're going to have to date her—woo her."

"Woo her? I'm a small-town shifter cop who spends most of his days driving alone in my car or talking to Miss Mabel on Main Street." Miss Mabel was ninety-five and refused to run her bakery any less than seven days a week.

"Remember how I made Ava promise to be mine, and then had to work my ass off to win her over?" How could I forget? "Well, that's you now. Win her over."

He made it sound so easy when there were hundreds of miles between us. "You think asking her on a date will solve all this?"

"Do something to show her you like her. She turned you down, you left. I'm sure she thinks you're there for the baby and because she knows about us."

"Which is why I'm here." I wasn't being willfully dense, but I hadn't wanted to push myself onto a woman and I'd had to come here and do just that.

"Ava's told me a bit about Avril's life, and it didn't

sound like she had anybody. Maybe that's what terrifies her the most about moving to a town where there's no real career options for her, and you're working all the time. Ava and Venus are happily mated, and she's afraid she won't even have you. You need to start building trust, at the very least. From there, maybe you two can build a real relationship."

I scrubbed my face. Deacon's sensible words were like an arrow of terror straight into my soul. "She's going to be forced to move to Silver Lake to raise our baby."

"Then prove it won't be everything she feared. The difference between Silver Lake and where she grew up is you."

These were the moments I disliked my brother. When his oldest-sibling confidence wouldn't let me back down. As the next youngest, that type of attitude usually motivated me. I let the determination flow through me, fueling each cell, drawing on the recent experience of my brothers with their females. They had each fought an uphill battle to win their mates. I had better get started.

AVRIL

I GOT HOME from work and all I wanted to do was collapse into bed. My emotions were on the third loop of the Wild Thing hypercoaster in my head, and I wanted to bury my face in the pillow and cry.

A lot of people gushed about how rewarding a nursing career was, but there wasn't nearly enough discussion about the tough days or how to deal with them when you were out of the unit and your adrenaline plummets. The silence of the car could make what happened on the shift seem worse or better. Some mornings after a grueling night shift, not even the sun could chase the shadows away.

I parked in the garage and walked into the condo, greeted by the familiar savory smells of an omelet. My stomach immediately rumbled. Steel appeared at the top of the stairs, looking like he'd had as rough a night as I'd had.

"Morning," I greeted wearily.

He came down the stairs and met me at the landing, taking the bag I'd packed with my lunch, my water bottles, and slipped the backpack off my shoulder. "I made you some food."

He waited for me to go up the stairs. As tired as I was, my fatigue lifted when I spotted a big old plate of cheesy omelet. The food suddenly became my sole focus. I sat down, gripped the fork, and all concerns of propriety were gone. I shoveled food into my mouth, chewed and swallowed. I downed the glass of orange juice, and it was replaced by another as I attacked what was left on the plate.

When I was done, I put my fork down with a groan. "That was so good." It was like a fog lifted and I focused on Steel. The satisfied glint was back in his eye, the one that he usually got when he saw me eating. The one that was quickly becoming my favorite look on him, other than shirtless or naked. "Thank you."

"No problem. Do you want to wind down before bed?" He briefly closed his eyes. "I meant, do you need to wind down? I wasn't coming on to you." The gray in his eyes darkened. "Unless you want me to."

"No." With my hunger satiated, the emotions of my night flooded back. Hot tears pricked the backs of my eyes.

He was at my side in an instant. Tears spilled down my cheeks and he captured each one with the pad of his thumb. The onslaught was too much for him to keep up with. He gathered me in his arms and carried me to the bedroom. He set me on my feet to pull the sheet back, and I crawled in on autopilot. I thought he would tuck me in and leave, but he didn't. He rounded the bed and dropped his pants.

"What are you doing?" The shock of being faced with his powerful thighs was enough to stem the flow of tears.

"I stayed up all night so I could sleep when you slept. I can go down to the guest room, but I just want to hold you right now."

Moisture welled in my eyes again. "Why?"

"Because you need it. And I want to."

Either answer would've worked; both of them together were perfect. I nodded and let the tears fall. I was tempted to give him an excuse about how I wasn't usually this emotional. I had cried in front of him yesterday, and I was bawling again today. Both times for good reason, and I refused to apologize for it.

But the thing was, I didn't feel like I had to justify my emotions around him. With Ian, I would've. He'd have gotten fidgety and complained about not knowing what to do or what to tell me, as if it was my problem he didn't know how to react.

Steel didn't say anything as he gathered me in his arms. I rolled over and burrowed into his chest. My body shook as I cried. His warm hands rubbed up and down my back, and he made sure his hips were far enough away that I didn't feel a single ounce of sexual pressure in the moment.

When no more tears came, my breathing evened out. I blinked, sniffled, and wiped my face. "A patient died today. She'd been in ICU for three weeks. None of us thought she'd make it, and she didn't, but that doesn't make me feel better."

"I'm sorry. Doesn't it seem odd that every single person in the world dies, but we're never really taught how to deal with it?"

I looked at him through my tear-laden lashes. "It's the same for shifters?"

He nodded. "I could make up something like we have sacred altars and special ceremonies, but those have fallen by the wayside now that we've lived among humans for so long."

"Some deaths are easier than others." I winced. "That's fucked up to say."

"No, it makes sense. Some people leave more behind than others."

He hadn't taken his shirt off. He probably didn't want to make me uncomfortable but hadn't wanted to crawl into bed with his pants, yet I wished he had completely stripped down. "You have to deal with death a lot? Oh, right. The executions."

His embrace tightened for a moment. "Shifters can heal from a lot of wounds, but we still have mental problems. Fights and domestic disputes. Murders and accidental killings. I try to take care of those so they don't reach Deacon."

I ran my fingertips down his face, loving the roughness of his stubble. "Protective little brother."

My stomach was full, and my mind was at peace

thanks to the crying. Warm tingles slowly spread through my body, smothering all talk of death and growing in frequency.

"I didn't come in here to seduce you, Avril." He gripped my hand in his and brought it to his mouth, feathering his lips over my fingers. "I want to, I will always want to, but you're tired, and you need rest."

He would always want me. "Say it again." I didn't know why I needed to hear it.

"You need to rest."

"No, before that."

"You're tired," he said with a playful note. When I scowled at him, he softly chuckled. "I want you, Avril. Always. There's something between us and that circle of issues you mentioned yesterday goes around that, but it doesn't change that I want to sink into you every chance I get."

I had come home after a long night of work to a guy who had switched his hours around and made me breakfast, then held me while I cried. He admitted he desired me. The attraction wasn't one sided. Something had shifted between us, and I only wanted to let it comfort me after a hard shift.

"Can you stay and talk with me? I don't know if I can fall asleep, but I don't want to get out of bed."

"I'd be happy to." He tucked me farther into the cocoon of his body. Even without what happened during the night, I wouldn't want to be anywhere else. "Did you always know you wanted to be a nurse?"

"No. But I was able to get a scholarship for it. No matter where I moved to, I knew there would always be jobs, and the pay is decent."

He buried his nose in my hair and inhaled. He would

do that when we were together before. I had asked him once if my hair smelled good, and he said that I reminded him of the peonies his grandma used to plant. Bold, fragrant, and full of life. I liked the flower, but I also knew they were top-heavy and had a very short season. That had seemed more fitting than Steel's description.

"If you could do it over again, what would you be?" He had moved a hand to my hip and was absentmindedly stroking me. Everything with this guy could be considered sexual.

I focused on his question. "I don't know. I like nursing. I like working in the hospital—the pace and the novel environment. I don't know, maybe I would've chosen nursing no matter what. But sometimes, I get so frustrated working with doctors."

"Why?"

"Different personalities. They aren't all good with the patients and when they aren't, I get the blowback."

"Would you have rather gone to med school?"

I shook my head, and it had the effect of snuggling deeper into his body. Or maybe I was using any movement as an excuse to cuddle closer to him. "No, definitely not. I could go back to school and become a nurse practitioner or something, but I can't afford it. Plus, I'm going to have a baby. It would be a lot to take on."

He paused midstroke and resumed a moment later. I knew what he was thinking but was grateful he didn't say it. If I had nothing else to do in Silver Lake, he would be there to help with the baby. But he'd said his people healed quickly, so there wasn't much work for a nurse practitioner in Silver Lake.

I turned the topic around on him. "Did you have to do what you're doing now?"

He paused his hand again. He flattened his palm on my hip. "One of our family has always taken the position. Ruling families tend to have more than one kid. Like I told you, we're all born with abilities that serve our people, but we're also there to serve and protect our ruler."

"No coup on your watch?"

"That's one reason. Deacon's a good ruler. Strong and fair. He's the best thing for the clan, and it's my job to keep him in his position."

There was something about the way he described what he did for a living. He was missing passion. He was all about duty. He might like his job, but we were sort of alike in that aspect. We did what we did because we had to. Wanting to wasn't high on the priority list. "If you could go back and pick anything, what would it be?"

His fingers resumed lazy circles on my hip. "I never thought about it." He nuzzled my hair again. "That's not quite correct. I never thought about it in those terms. But sometimes, since I interact with a lot of humans regularly, and we live in a human world, it would be handy to know more about the law than I do."

"You want to be a lawyer?"

His hand went still again. For a guy who didn't say much, his body spoke loud and clear. I learned as much about how he was feeling through his touch as from what he said. "Yeah, I wanted to go to law school."

"Is that a possibility?"

"No, not really. Maybe if I had gone right out of school, but I'm not leaving the clan right after Deacon mated. He and Ava might start having kids, and our clan is really stable, but I don't want to take any chances."

He was willing to sacrifice what he wanted for his brother and for his people. It made my unwillingness to move to Silver Lake seem selfish. But I didn't have a choice anymore. The fatigue returned with a vengeance.

"Steel, I'm going to go to sleep now. Can you hold me until I fall asleep?"

"I'll hold you as long as you let me," he murmured. And I knew he wasn't talking about just today.

CHAPTER
SIX

S teel

Sleeping during the day sucked. I didn't know how Avril did it. I couldn't sleep as deeply as I was used to, and every hour on the hour, I'd wake up.

I had made good on my promise to hold her while she slept, but I'd had to let her go to keep from waking her with my tossing and turning. I slept well enough that I could stay in bed, otherwise I would've left the bedroom to keep from disturbing her.

Her breathing changed when she woke. She let out a sigh and rolled onto her back. When she saw I was awake, she blinked. "How did you sleep?"

"Shitty. You?"

"Same." She let out another sigh and stretched her arms over her head. "Sometimes I get up for a while, and then take a nap before my shift starts."

"And you do this for three days?"

"Six. It's like two weeks butted together. But then I'll get a week off."

Six days of sleeping like this sounded like a nightmare. But I was in bed with Avril, that was further than I thought we would get when I first arrived.

"Oof, the baby's dancing on my bladder. I've gotta go to the bathroom again. Be right back."

I took that as an order to stay in bed. She disappeared into the bathroom, and when she was done, she crawled right back into bed. She lay on her back and threw her arms above her head again. My gaze was drawn to her waist. Our baby was in there.

She caught me looking. "Steel?"

"It just hit me," I said gruffly. "I've been so worried about you and how you'd react to everything that I never had a chance to stop and think... that's our child."

She rolled her shirt up to bare her stomach and rolled the waistband of her shorts down to her pubic bone. "That's our child."

"Can I... touch you?" I didn't know how to ask. She was only a couple months along, and the baby was so tiny, but the drive to feel it was undeniable.

"Yes," she said as if she realized this was our first time acknowledging more than the—as Deacon called it— logistics of the kid.

I scooted down to the middle of the bed so my face could be level with her rounded abdomen. I loved her curves, and I couldn't wait to see her belly grow big with our young. I'd grown up knowing I'd have to mate by the time I was thirty-five, but I wasn't yet thirty-three. Old enough to wonder if it'd happen. Without that special someone, I hadn't thought about a family. Kids. Backyard barbecues and lawn games. Lazy mornings with children bouncing on the bed, asking us when we were going to get up, like my brothers and I had done with our parents.

I hadn't been able to admit how badly I wanted it until now.

Bypassing the tentative touch, I laid my hand flat on her belly. She sucked in a breath, held it for a heartbeat, then let it out.

I had my hand on the woman who would soon become my mate and who was carrying our child. This moment was almost perfect. If only she wanted to be with me as much as I wanted her.

"Avril." Inching closer, I laid my head on her stomach.

She tangled her fingers in my hair, and we rested like that for several minutes. Her quiet breathing was interspersed with the natural gurgles in her body. In six months, I'd be able to hear the heartbeat of our child. She would only be able to hear it when she had her ultrasound, but my hearing was more acute. I'd lay my head against her like this and hear the steady thump.

Goddamn, I couldn't wait.

"What are you thinking?" she asked.

My thoughts would terrify her. I was a male obsessed. She and this baby were the center of my world, and it was a world she didn't want to be in at all. A world she would be forced to live in. "That I really want to make you happy."

"You're not responsible for my happiness."

"But I could be responsible for your unhappiness." Without thinking, I pressed a kiss to her belly. "The happiness of you and this child has become the most important thing to me."

"I wish that was true, Steel."

The same argument. I went back to what Deacon said. She didn't trust me. Not yet.

I dropped another kiss on her stomach. My duty was important, but how did I show her she wasn't excluded? We were shifters. Protecting our kind came first and foremost, otherwise we wouldn't be able to live the life we wanted with the ones we loved. We did what we did for them, and I would do it for her.

Her fingers tightened in my hair. She didn't tell me to stop. The issues between us weren't a concrete wall, if just for a while. I pressed another kiss on her soft skin. Her peony scent bloomed stronger.

I groaned and curled my fingers around her waistband. "I can smell how turned on you are, Avril."

"We shouldn't do this." Her words came out breathy, heavy with need.

No, we weren't ready to have sex yet. I wanted too much from her she wasn't ready to give. "I just want to make you feel good. No more."

She licked her lips, and her pink tongue captivated me. "What about you?"

"I'll get enough pleasure when you scream my name as you come."

Her legs relaxed and widened automatically. That was enough of a confirmation for me.

I rolled her shorts off and spread her knees. Blood pounded through my erection, but I was content to suffer as long as I got to taste her again.

Sinking between her thighs, I kissed the apex of each leg. "Remember the first time I did this?"

"How could I forget?" she groaned and rolled her hips up, a silent plea for me to get busy. But I'd been dreaming of being in this exact position for two months, I wasn't rushing it.

"You tasted so fucking sweet. You smell like flowers, but your flavor is all saltwater taffy. You know how much fucking taffy I have eaten in the last two months?"

She tugged my head closer to her center, but I resisted. My impatient human would have to wait. She relented. "How much?"

"Not enough. Because it wasn't you." And with that, I feasted. My resistance went out the window as soon as her flavor was back on my tongue. I boasted about not rushing, but I felt like I was in the race of my life.

She didn't take her hands out of my hair, and she kept her knees hitched up, giving me as much access as possible. I wasn't the only one suffering since we'd been apart.

This thing between us wasn't an accident. We didn't plan to have a baby together, but this woman was mine. She fit me in so many ways. I could be everything she wanted; she just had to give me a chance.

If I was heartless enough to use sex to convince her, I would. But the truth was, I was helpless. I would take as much as she would give me, and like a stray dog, I would sit outside her door, begging for more.

She came apart. My name echoed off the walls as she bowed her back to keep from releasing my hair. I kept licking lazy circles around her clit. I hadn't even gotten to put a finger inside of her. I wanted more, and I hoped to hell that she did too.

She went boneless into the mattress. I slowed the rhythm of my tongue, but I continued to lick through her sweet juices. "Steel, I don't think I can come again."

I paused only to say, "Do you want to find out?"

Intrigue shone in her dull-brown eyes. She knew I

could get her off again. I'd proven it already. The decision was hers. "What about you?"

The warmth inside me had nothing to do with the fire of lust raging through my blood. My dick was as hard as concrete. One look from her and I would probably explode. But I hadn't lied to her earlier. Her pleasure was my pleasure. Two orgasms should give her a decent nap before she worked tonight. "Let me do this for you."

She hesitated a moment before she nodded.

And I returned to my happy place. Between her legs, feasting on her. The whimpers she made were like a symphony in my ears, and the way her body writhed with nothing but simple circles from my tongue was addictive.

Her hips pumped like she needed something to ride. I thrust a finger into her and groaned when her hot, wet heat clamped around me. She hadn't held back before, but her climax had hit as quick as lightning.

This orgasm was going to mess up the bed. Her body was like a wave as she rode my face. Her hands fisted and twisted in the sheets, and she alternated between propping her heels on my shoulders and planting them into the mattress.

She might have a good nap, but I would have to take five cold showers before I had any chance of sleep.

This time when she came, it was a slow buildup with a gradual explosion, no less powerful, but more harmonious. She climaxed on a sigh, my name falling from her lips, and when she crested her peak, I backed off.

I crawled up her body, and she watched me through half-lidded eyes.

"The night shift doesn't seem so bad right now," she murmured. Dancing her fingers over my shirt, she worked her way down. "You said this was for me, but you've got to be uncomfortable."

"Get some rest, Avril." I grabbed her fingers and kissed her knuckles. "That was for you."

Her lips formed a brief pout before her fatigue won out. "Okay, but tomorrow it's your turn." Her eyelids drifted shut.

Her bottom half was still naked. I covered her up and tucked her in. I'd worry about the cleanup when she woke later and jumped in the shower. For now, I was content to watch my future mate and hope she realized that this thing between us was more than duty.

AVRIL

MY LAST NIGHT shift was tonight. The days had flown by. But then having marathon oral sex in between stretches of sleep did that to a person.

I had Steel in the middle of my bed, with his legs splayed and his muscles straining. I deep throated him with my ass in the air. The vanity mirror on the dresser across from my bed showed him everything. Like the other times before, I would die of mortification when I realized the view he actually got, but I also knew how much he loved it. It was empowering in the moment, death by embarrassment afterward.

But we were definitely in the moment. Both of us were stripped down. He'd already gone down on me, and after that first day in bed, I refused to let him go without his own release.

He buried a hand in my hair, but he didn't push or shove my head or direct me in any way. The only obvious opinion he had about the blow jobs I gave was enthusiastic participation. He didn't critique me. And he didn't tell me about past experiences of women who'd given him head. I put my mouth on him and he orgasmed. It was as simple as that.

If I thought about my other experiences too hard, rage would sweep me away like a summer tornado. I had put up with some shitty treatment in the past. I was going to lose the life I had built for myself in the near future, but in this, Steel gave me everything I needed.

"Fuck, Avril. I can't look at you and not see those full lips wrapped around my cock."

He liked to talk dirty. I liked hearing it. I hummed over his length.

"When I see your dripping-wet pussy in the air, it makes me feral. I want to bury my face in you and lick you up till there's nothing left."

He'd done that. After five days of his head between my thighs, I was surprised I could even walk to the car to get to work.

His hot length throbbed in my mouth. I hummed again, only because I knew he liked it, and when I did it right before he was ready to orgasm, his entire body went rigid.

"Fuck, woman. That mouth is my dream come true."

We hadn't had sex yet. As if what we'd been doing hadn't been intimate, sex still seemed like it was too far, too fast. My future was him. My child was his. His hometown would be mine. It was like I was hugging this one thing to myself for as long as possible.

And Steel never made me feel like I had to go further than I was comfortable.

That thought filled me with an unidentifiable emotion I didn't care to inspect too closely. I redoubled my efforts, and he came with a roar. It was a heady experience. All that raw power captured by my mouth. He was over six feet of chiseled muscle and he was rigid underneath me, trying not to thrust so hard he hurt me.

I swallowed him down, waiting until his movements slowed before I took my mouth off him. Prowling up his body, I tucked myself into his side. He stayed sprawled across the bed, but the arm that banded around me held me close.

We lay like that for several minutes. Usually it was a comfortable silence, but my mind was whirling with emotions.

I liked Steel. And the longer he was around, the more I liked him. I first had sex with him because he was hot. The sex was amazing, and we kept doing it until he had to leave. Now that he was back, it wasn't just his looks, or how he could strum orgasm after orgasm out of me.

He asked how work was. We talked about deep issues. Do-not-resuscitate orders, uncaring family, heartbroken family, asshole doctors, supportive doctors, end of life, the cost of school, everything. Not once had he discussed for an hour what the best protein shake flavor was. Nothing was wrong with Ian's passions, it was just that he was never interested in mine.

The more I talked with Steel, the more I fell for him. I was already giving up everything. I couldn't give up my heart too. I couldn't turn out like my mother. My baby was going to get better from me.

"What do you want to eat before work?" His deep

rumble went through his chest and into my ear. If he could sense the struggle inside me, he didn't address it.

"Meat."

He chuckled, and I smiled against his warm skin. "How's tomorrow going to go? Are we going to stay up all day so you can switch hours around?"

I roused myself out of my postcoital delirium. "Yes. I'll stay awake the whole day. I'll have a week off, and then I start a stretch of day shifts."

"Can I stay with you for the week? Then when you go back to work, I'll go back to Silver Lake for a while."

I hid my frown in his warm side. He was leaving?

Of course he was. He had a life and career in a whole different town that hadn't included me before he found out I was pregnant. "That sounds like a good plan."

His arm tightened. "Or you could come with me during your days off, and then I could stay with you while you worked to prep your meals and stuff."

It was everything I could do to keep from nodding. That plan sounded much better.

No. I wasn't going to Silver Lake before I had to. I had told Ava and Venus about my pregnancy. I wasn't strutting around a tiny town where they could talk about my circumstances. I wasn't yet three months along. "It's early yet. I don't want to go public before the first trimester."

"Okay." A simple reply, but uttered so quietly I knew he'd had a hard time hiding his disappointment.

"Okay." It was decided. No one said making the best decisions for myself would be easy, but I had no idea how hard it would be.

CHAPTER
SEVEN

S teel

THE WEEK AVRIL had off had gone by way too fast, and it had been cut short by two days. Her supervisor had called, asking her to fill in for a couple of days. Time and a half, Avril claimed. I could cash in one of the gemstones from my hoard and give her the money. It would be more than what she would make in those two shifts. But the decision had been hers, and she made it.

I wasn't sure if she wanted to work, if she felt she had to, or if she needed a break from me.

We'd been sleeping together and doing everything in bed together except for full-fledged sex. We didn't leave her bed. It was as if there was an unspoken rule—only oral sex and only on a mattress.

I could understand why going all the way would overwhelm her after everything she'd learned in the last couple of weeks, but I didn't understand why we were restricted to the bedroom. I just had a strong feeling I shouldn't make any moves on her outside of that room.

But I pondered the reasons on my drive back to Silver Lake. Staying in bed with her had seemed like a fantasy. What they called a staycation. Perhaps if we had moved to other places in her condo, like we had done a couple of months ago, then maybe it would seem too real for her.

We'd get there. I had to have faith in that.

I pulled into a spot in front of city hall. Deacon's pickup was already there. He said he'd wait until I had arrangements made with Avril before he discussed my situation with the council, which I appreciated. Like Avril said, it was early yet.

I found Deacon in his office with his head bent over papers on the desk. They were likely contracts since he was officially a mayor and had all the paperwork to go along with the job.

He looked up when I came to the door. "Hey, I wasn't sure if you were actually coming back."

"You know I have to."

"I meant before the baby—" He lifted his chin toward the door. I closed it, but we'd have to keep our voices low. I didn't want any shifters in the building overhearing my conversation.

"I need to talk to you about commuting back and forth for a while."

Deacon studied me until I started to squirm. "It's not going well?" He was my brother. He wouldn't be swayed by a neutral answer or tolerate me evading the subject. Not only was Avril literally his business, but he took his older-brother role seriously.

"I don't have to tell you." I said it without heat. I

didn't want to talk about it, mostly because I didn't know what to say. *Avril and I are having incredible oral sex and if I can convince her clit a future with me won't turn her into her mother, then I'm good.*

He spread his hands. "You're right. But I'm concerned about you. You didn't exactly dance in here on a cloud of excitement."

I let out a heavy breath and sat forward in the chair, resting my elbows on my thighs. "She's holding back. It's going to take time, and she asked for time, so…"

"So, you're stuck commuting back and forth."

I nodded, dropping my gaze to the hardwood floor. "I've already missed a lot of work."

"You can stay with her until the baby's born. Babies can't shift, and Mathilda can get to know her after she moves here." Mathilda was the town's midwife. She was getting up there in age and was recruiting any willing body she could to be her successor.

"I don't want to smother her either." I was walking a tightrope, only her life was on the line, not mine.

"Distance makes the heart grow fonder?"

"Fuck, I hope so, but I'm not commuting to play games."

He studied me, but I stayed sprawled in his chair. I was antsy to get out and patrol. Talk to Miss Mabel to get the lowdown on what had happened while I was gone. Deacon might've suppressed any issues from the town or the council to keep me from rushing back, but Miss Mabel would give it to me straight.

"Why didn't I know how you felt about her when she came to my place? Or when we were in Minnesota?"

"I didn't need you thinking that I was using her."

"I know better."

"Ava doesn't. And Venus might seem like she's mellowed out, but I have a strong suspicion she would've threatened a body part I quite enjoy having if I hurt Avril." Ava and Venus couldn't have known he had no power when it came to Avril. She held his balls in the palm of her hand.

And after the last couple of weeks, that was exactly where he preferred them. He rose before those memories made sitting in his brother's office uncomfortable. "I'd better get on the clock. Don't want anyone thinking they can misbehave while I'm trying to win Avril over."

Sarcasm laced his voice when he said, "Tell Miss Mabel hi."

"Will do." I'd stop at my place first and change—and grab a handful of taffy.

~

AVRIL

I JUGGLED MY TOTE BAG, my lunch pack, and my water bottle as I let myself into the condo. My phone started buzzing.

Inside, I dropped everything and looked at the caller. Ava. I messaged her and Venus regularly, but since she called, Steel must've returned to Silver Lake.

"Hey," I answered as I grabbed everything I could in one hand and brought it to the kitchen while talking to her.

"How are you feeling?"

Hungry. Like I wanted to vibrate out of my skin. And cranky, like it was the day before that time of the month started and everyone annoyed me. Only times ten. Apparently the orgasms neutralized the crankiness. "I'm fine. Living the dream."

I paused as I set my lunch bag on the counter. This wasn't my dream. But at the same time, it was. I had wanted a job where I could make enough money to support myself. I had it. But that was all I did. I didn't go to the gym anymore. I hadn't felt the need while I was doing gymnastics for hours in bed with Steel. After work, I was too tired to think about driving anywhere but home.

Without Steel, coming home didn't excite me as much as it used to.

Ava snapped me out of my head. "You're feeling good? Everything is good with the baby?"

"All is well. But that's not what you called for."

"I'm always thinking about you and my little niece or nephew."

A smile chased away my doldrums. She would've been my baby's aunt no matter what, but since she was mated to Deacon, she really would be an aunt.

"But to get back to your point," she said, "yes, I wanted to talk to you about how it's going with Steel. Deacon talked to him. You're not moving here until the baby's born?" She tried to keep the disappointment out of her voice, but I knew her well enough to hear it.

"Is that going to be an issue?" What if it was? What would I do? What would Steel do?

"It didn't sound like it. They have a midwife here. I met her once at the bakery, and I think you'd like her, but Deacon said it's not critical the baby's born in the clan, just that it'll be raised here. I just don't know why all of this bothers you. And that's why I am worried."

Because she thought I was grappling for any source of control I could. Was she wrong? "I don't want to leave my job until I have to."

I bit my lip like I caught myself lying. I did like my job. But I wasn't looking forward to going to work tomorrow and learning the patient in room 301 had taken a turn for the worse. Her husband had been by her side for days, and I think she was waiting for him to leave before she could go.

The circle of life was exhausting and I witnessed the end more than I cared to. I thought the intensity of ICU would be invigorating, but it weighed me down as if my scrubs were lined with lead. Oncology always had openings, but it took more than I was willing to give to work in that unit. Peds—same. Mom and baby were always full, and it took knowing someone to get in. I had been eyeing a labor and delivery opening, but then Ian—and then Steel.

But there wasn't even a clinic in Silver Lake, so I would work as long as I could before I became dependent on Steel.

"You worked hard for your degree," she agreed.

"I did." And as of last August, I had worked the three years required to fulfill my scholarship requirement. I had accomplished what I set out to do, but I hadn't even treated myself to an extra treat from the hospital café.

I opened the fridge door and peered inside. Neatly stacked meals lined the shelves. They were all heat and serve. I didn't have to lift a finger to do any of the work for breakfast, lunch, or dinner. My lunches were neatly stacked on the bottom shelf—labeled for the days I worked, for fuck's sake. Everything was precooked and prepackaged. And it was all delicious. I wouldn't have to stop at the grocery store all week, and that used to be the bane of my existence. I hated getting home, taking my bra off, and then realizing I was out of an ingredient I needed to make supper.

Ava let out a gusty sigh. "I want to tell you stuff like 'Steel will treat you right,' but I know how inane that is. It just minimizes everything you're going through while I'm selfishly looking forward to living in the same town as my best friend again."

I chuckled. The major bonus to Silver Lake—two bonuses, really—are Ava and Venus.

Steel would treat me right. Wasn't that what a lot of girls hoped for when they grew up? Find that one special person who treated them decently. The bar was set pretty low these days. Otherwise, Ian wouldn't have looked like such a catch. Staring at all the labeled food containers that would take me through each day I worked while Steel was gone made me wonder how in the world I had missed so many red flags with my ex.

"You know what really sucks?" The containers inside the fridge rattled when I slammed the door shut. "Is that in any other situation Steel would be such a catch. I mean, I don't know him that well, but a guy can't be that good in bed, and that considerate keeping the mother of his baby well fed, without lacking in other areas. I've met his brothers, and his brothers' wives—mates—whatever, are my best friends. Steel should be fucking perfect. But the shitty men who came before him ruined it." And one of them was my dad.

"They haven't ruined anything, Avril," Ava said gently. "Without Ian, you're finally able to heal. Maybe it makes you uncomfortable that being with Steel shows you just how badly you and your mother were treated. You've lived over twenty years doing everything you can not to be your mom. Those feelings won't change overnight."

I slumped against the counter again and pinched the bridge of my nose. "Are you sure you want to go into accounting? You'd make a better counselor."

She chuckled. "I'm not going to any more schooling. This CPA stuff is giving me a headache."

"Well, you'd be good. I need to hang on to a part of myself. I need that life preserver in the background. When Ian left, I would've been a mess for days without Venus. And Ian didn't even live here with me. The asshole had mooched off me for years. I spent a lot of time with him, but I didn't have his baby, we weren't married, and when he left, it still crushed me. And now with Steel…"

"What if you can trust him?"

"Isn't that the problem? You don't know if you can trust someone until they hurt you. I'm glad you're happy and all. Venus is delirious in love. But I'm not her. I'm not you. And I don't know Steel."

"I am deliriously happy. But we had an argument just last week. I hollered at him. He raised his voice because he thought I was overreacting. But we work through it. That's what relationships are about."

She fought with Deacon? They might be a thing, but their relationship wasn't even six months old. "What was the fight over?"

She made a disgusted sound. "It was silly. He started tearing up the front yard for landscaping without asking me. He had it all planned already, no input from me. But every day he tells me his house is my house too."

I could see how that would bother her. She had left our hometown and moved in with a guy. Then he kicked her out, and she'd basically been homeless. So when she'd lost her job right after, that was the last of my best friend living in the same town as me. She'd gone back home, went fishing with her dad, which led her to Deacon, and the rest was history. "But now he's doing exactly what you want for landscaping."

"Actually, his plans looked pretty nice. I threw a fit over nothing."

"If it was nothing, you wouldn't have reacted the way you did."

"I know. And he knows that too. But I didn't call to talk about me."

Hearing her story helped. "I haven't seen many healthy relationships."

"You grew up seeing my parents."

Right. I did. Ava's mom died a few years ago and her dad hadn't dragged himself into a bottle. A lingering sadness would remain in his eyes, but he lived his life, laughed a lot, and loved his daughter fiercely. "They were a good couple."

"One of the best. There are good guys out there. I'm glad you're at least giving Steel a chance."

"I don't know if you'd call it a chance." If I'd been willing to do that, we'd have sex again. When he got that hot gleam in his eye while we were eating at the island, I would've let him lift me onto the counter and strip me down. We would've had sex on the island like we did when we'd been having sex before. So, honestly, I didn't know what I was doing with Steel other than playing with fire. Standing on the edge of a cliff with a stiff wind at my back. "He's got to be in my life no matter what. I guess that's where we're at."

"He told Deacon he's going back out there in a few days."

"I guess." Butterflies kicked up in my belly. I looked forward to seeing him again, to being back in his arms. Ava would never know from my tone.

"Okay, keep in touch. I'm still going to worry about you."

"I'll worry about you." I wouldn't. I'd seen Deacon around her enough to know that nothing was going to get to Ava if he had any control over it.

I could lie and say I didn't want that. That I wanted to be a strong, independent woman who didn't need a man. But I could be strong and independent and capable of being on my own, and still want a partner in life.

And a large part of me wanted Steel to be more than a partner. And that was the part I was driven to protect.

CHAPTER

EIGHT

S teel

I HAD JUST FINISHED PACKING the last of my items to return to Minneapolis when my phone rang. I dropped onto the bed next to my bag and answered the number I didn't recognize. "Hello?"

"Steel Silver?"

"Yeah?" I didn't recognize the older woman on the other end. I knew everyone in town, but hearing them talk on the phone was a different experience.

"Can you—what I'm asking—" A loud, gusty sigh came over the line. "I was told to call you the next time my neighbors started arguing."

The sinking sensation in my stomach was new. Usually, I was up and out the door, ready to do my job. I didn't mind quiet and boring days in my line of work. If things got exciting, that too often meant someone I knew was getting hurt. I had never actively wanted to shirk my duties like I did now. But did the call have to come in minutes before I planned to leave town?

I scrubbed my face. Yes, otherwise Deacon would have to deal with it. "What's going on with your neighbors?"

"She's screaming—they argue all the time—but I heard glass breaking. My kids told me the next time I heard them arguing like that I should call you."

"What's the address?"

She rattled off the address to a place on the other side of Silver Lake from where my brother lived.

Leaving my duffel bag behind, I locked up and went out to my car. A flutter of anxiety curled through my blood. Ever since I'd been shot doing a check on the Garnet River ferals, I experienced more trepidation than usual. Dread mined into my bones. A natural byproduct of the trauma I had gone through, but annoying nonetheless.

I kicked the car into gear. I was a shifter, watching over a town full of shifters. I shouldn't feel the need to wear a bulletproof vest, and especially not carry a handgun. Unless it was deer season, I didn't want anything to do with guns. Shifters had stricter laws about turning guns on each other than humans did. Too many risks. The biggest one was turning into a dragon in front of human eyes. Bullet wounds didn't make a shifter logical.

The little development I turned into had seven houses on lots that were two to eight acres big. Shifters had good hearing, but how loud was this couple screaming at each other if the little old lady could hear it?

I spotted the house that supposedly had the arguing couple. To the right, separated by a row of lilacs was the caller's place. That house was just as quiet, but the woman would be prudent to keep her head low. As long as she didn't tell anyone, no one would hear it from me she had reported the argument.

I parked in front of the place in question. Eerie silence had descended around the neighborhood. The screen door was closed on the house, but the main door hung open. The lingering smell of fury, terror, and anguish hung in the air.

My dread magnified. Shit. I took the steps to the screen door, hearing no sounds inside.

The muscles of my back tensed as if in preparation for taking another high-powered rifle round. The scars were gone, but the memory of their wounds throbbed beneath my shirt.

Knocking on the door, I called, "Anyone home?"

The metallic tang of blood slapped my nose. Without thinking, I pushed inside. The sight that greeted me made me want to sink to my knees and wrap my head in my hands. But there was no mourning on the job. And unfortunately, this wasn't the first domestic dispute I had come upon that had ended horribly.

Her name was Darcy. She wasn't going to recover from the wounds ripped into her throat and the rest of her body. Few shifters were strong enough to recover from a sudden and massive blood loss like that.

I crouched next to her and scanned the rest of the house. I would have to search it, make sure there were no kids and no one else, though I didn't recall Darcy and her mate Michael having young yet. Michael was closer to Penn's age, and he'd always been a hothead. He had kept wanting to resurrect our clan's beef with Jade even after

Lachlan had taken over and things had mellowed out with Jade clan.

Slowly, I rose. The house was as silent as death. A quick sweep of the place showed me it was empty. Michael had run. He knew what he'd done had earned him an instant termination. Our laws were stricter and executed more swiftly than human laws.

Michael was the type of guy who had been looking for a fight his entire life, and it had just earned him the death penalty.

I slammed out the front door and stalked down the front steps and the sidewalk to my pickup. My mind settled into hunt mode as I stripped out of my clothing and dumped my belongings into the back seat. Slamming the door, I headed straight for the trees circling the property. There was nothing but woods around Silver Lake, and Michael knew these woods as well as I did.

I sensed movement behind me, but a quick glance over my shoulder showed me the woman who called had stepped onto her porch. Her name and details ran through my mind, but they were insignificant. I had a job to do. Terminating Michael took priority, and I wouldn't quit until he was as gone as his mate inside the house. Until then, he was a danger to our people. I couldn't quit until this grim task was completed.

～

AVRIL

WHEN I HAD GOTTEN home from work yesterday, Steel hadn't been here. I had no messages, and he hadn't called. I'd spent the evening thinking he'd show any minute. But he hadn't messaged either.

It was morning now and I'd had the worst night of sleep I'd had in a while. And my screen was still blank. Trying to get ready for the day, I leaned over my bathroom counter, scowling at my phone.

Where was he? Why hadn't he gotten in touch? This wasn't like him.

Maybe it was? I didn't know him. It hadn't been how he acted , but he'd gone to his home and perhaps he had second thoughts about me. Perhaps he wanted space before he had to settle down with me.

Acid boiled up my throat. Ugh. This morning sickness could stop anytime. It had been worse during Steel's absence.

I ditched the bathroom. Eating something might settle my tummy. In the fridge, there was one more breakfast Steel had made me. Did he suspect he was going to be gone a day longer than he had planned?

I ate the bagel sandwich he made, then changed into my gym gear. It'd been too long since I worked out, and now that I had adjusted to a day schedule after the last week of work, I would take advantage of it.

It didn't take long to get to the gym, but once I arrived, I stared at the door. Why did I work out here when I thought of it as Ian's gym?

Scanning the parking lot, I stopped when I spotted Ian's sporty yellow car. My decision was made. It was a beautiful day, and it'd been a while since I'd gone on a plain old walk. I got plenty of steps at work, but it wasn't for pleasure.

There was a walking path close to the gym, and I checked my phone one last time before I hit the trail.

The asphalt path wound through a quiet suburb, but it was still outside of Minneapolis. Nothing like the small town I had grown up in. I heard more cars than birds, but after a few minutes of soaking up the sun I relaxed into my walk.

The only problem with walking alone was that I had nothing but the thoughts banging around in my head to keep me occupied. All the uncertainties I had from the last two months rose, but under the clear blue sky, they didn't seem as momentous.

The baby wasn't due until the first part of next year. Winter for Minnesota and in North Dakota where Silver Lake was. Did I want to move during that season when I could take advantage of the nicer weather during the summer and fall?

Was I trying to come up with excuses to leave earlier?

No, I had my job. I had maternity leave. Surely Steel and whatever powers that be in the shifter world would let me take the days I had earned for maternity leave and get paid. But ultimately, I didn't know.

I peeked at my phone. Only a **What's cooking?** message from Venus with baby bottle and pacifier emojis. She sent as many emojis as words when she messaged.

I hadn't seen her since I learned she was a dragon shifter. That explained the times I felt like she was holding back when she was talking about her life and Penn. This was the first time I had really thought about all the other shifters I had been surrounded by. People who were a part of my life besides Ava.

And they all lived in another state, a short distance away from each other. Why was I so determined to live in a suburb that meant nothing to me? I had chosen my condo because it was close to the hospital that had offered me the scholarship. I didn't know my neighbors. Or their names. The older couple in the unit to my left were gone most of the winter. The young couple across the street had kids and had upset Ian when they talked to him about how fast he drove down the block. They had avoided me after his temper tantrum.

But I was eight hours away from my mom here. Eight hours away from memories. And I never ran across anyone I grew up with unless I planned it, which I didn't, and Ava was the only person I still talked to.

The trailer house I grew up in had felt like a prison. I couldn't even claim my mom was a warden because she had never been around. And I had never gone looking for her, otherwise I was afraid I would end up on the doorstep of one of my classmates' houses. One of my classmates with married parents.

I checked my phone again. Nothing from Steel.

Letting out a frustrated growl, I spun on my heel and charged down the trail back to my car.

I punched in Ava's number and didn't give her a chance for a greeting. "What's up with Steel?"

"Oh, crap. I'm sorry. I didn't even think that he wasn't able to talk to you or I would've called."

My pace kicked up until I was speed walking like my supervisor was behind me, asking me to stay another hour. "Is he all right?"

"Yes. At least, I think so."

"You think so?" My pitch went high.

"He had to deal with a domestic, Avril." She lowered her voice. "There was a murder, and shifters don't have jail. Steel's hunting the guy who did it."

I slowed, my breathing heavy. Putting my free hand on my hip, I arched my back to get more air. I had a tiny nugget in my belly, but it was already pushing on my lungs. Either that, or it was all the rations Steel provided. "What do you mean, shifters don't have jails?"

"They can't risk it. Shifters, you know, shifting in close spaces. Or justifying why their jails resemble zoo cages. The only punishment is death."

Steel had talked about that, but I didn't correlate his information with other crimes. I stopped and frowned at the black asphalt. "Steel's going to kill him?"

"Is there anyone around you?"

I whipped my head around, but I was alone. "No. Are you telling me Steel has to hunt down a murderer?"

"Yes. Deacon heard about the death and went to help. They're the ruling family, so it's their job. And I think Steel handles a lot to keep Deacon from having to do it all."

I pressed my hand to my suddenly aching heart. Steel had told me about his job. His duty, but I hadn't realized the extent of it.

No jail. No guns. I knew the answer, but I still asked, "How does he..."

"As their dragon. No guns. No weapons. The laws of their people say they have to shift to carry out justice."

The details were so much more real now. "That's awful."

"That's their lives. For what it's worth, I'm sure he's upset he couldn't get back when he wanted."

"Do you think he's okay?" He had to be. Panic clawed up my throat. I wasn't prepared to be a single mother. I didn't want to trap a guy into marriage, only to have him decide I wasn't worth it and leave me destitute. But my dad was still out there somewhere. He was happy with his new family, and I was happy never talking to him. I rested my hand on my belly. What if our child didn't have that option?

"Deacon's helping him in the search. And when they're done, I don't know. It's not like they sit around and share their feelings about what happened. I don't know if he'll need some downtime, or if he'll hit the road as soon as possible."

Steel wasn't out in the woods alone. Deacon was helping him, and that had to mean they were both okay. Strength in numbers, right? And then what? He killed someone he probably knew, maybe someone he'd grown up with, and he showered and went about his business?

It didn't seem right. He'd held me through my grief after losing a patient. Who did that for him? "Well, if you see him, can you tell him to call me?"

"Avril, I'm sure that as soon as he's near his phone he'll call you before he even gets dressed."

My nerves unfurled a fraction with her words. After I hung up, I stared at my phone for a few moments. I glanced up. My car wasn't far away.

Determination set in, and I charged toward it. A decision was made—one that was on my terms, one that felt right.

When I got behind the wheel, I dialed my supervisor. "Hey... I need to talk to you."

CHAPTER
NINE

S teel

ROLLING MY SHOULDERS, I stretched my neck. I had been in my dragon form all day yesterday and through the night. I thought I would be a dragon for another twenty-four hours, but with Deacon's help, we flushed out Michael and swiftly dealt with him.

I was in my human form now, grimly staring at my bloodstained hands. My face and neck were probably covered in blood. What would Avril think?

I was taking her away from everything that was familiar to her, and I had alluded to this side of me. But stories were different from reality. The duty she held against me literally stained me red. Carrying out my job protecting this town too often meant taking a life. She was a nurse. She worked to save lives.

How would she deal with this?

"You okay?" Concern was etched across Deacon's face. Tiny dots of blood were scattered across his body. His dogged pursuit had driven Michael into my path. I had been the one to dole out the punishment.

"Yeah, I'm fine. Just wishing I wasn't here right now." And that I wouldn't have to drop this ugly business onto Avril's lap. Shit, I hadn't even called her. "Avril probably thinks I stood her up, or that I'm not coming back."

"I'm sure Ava's talked to her."

Ava telling Avril about what was going on might be worse than having it come from me. It would seem like I was hiding it, or like I'd chosen my work over her. Which I had.

Deacon and I picked our way over the rocky shore of Steel Lake, the town's namesake. After several minutes of washing the blood off, we were ready to head back to my pickup. Deacon had gathered my phone and clothing from my vehicle and put them in his pickup. He was parked closer to the tree line.

We trudged back to the woods. We had a few miles to walk, skirting the shores of the lake before we got to his vehicle. But it was less risk walking through the woods naked than around the shores of the lake. The lake was technically on Silver family land, but it was easier to prevent trouble.

The closer we got to our destination, the faster I walked. The only reason I didn't run was so I didn't get sweaty. I hadn't wanted to greet Avril covered in blood, but being sweaty and covered in dirt wasn't a good option either. I planned to jump in my pickup and take off. I had to stop for my duffel bag.

"I guess this answers my question of whether you're leaving right away." Deacon easily kept up with me. "I thought maybe you'd wait till morning since it's already getting late."

"I'll be two days late by the time I get there. I hope she'll at least answer the phone." If I hit the road now, I could get to her place shortly after midnight. I'd spend the whole time deciding whether I should sneak into her place to keep from waking her up or use the doorbell.

Finally, Deacon's pickup was in sight. I jogged the rest of the way and yanked open the back door. I snatched my phone from the top of my clothing pile.

I had a couple of messages from Penn. But only one from Avril.

My stomach plummeted. I reread her message five times before I jerked my gaze to Deacon as if he could tell me what was going on.

His gaze dropped to the phone. "That bad?"

"She told me not to come. She said to stay put."

"Why?"

I shook my head and stared at the message. **Stay put. Don't come here.** "Maybe because this whole thing just started between us and I've already had to pass her over for my job."

"Shit, Steel. I'm sorry. Eventually, she'll understand the needs of our life. You need that in a mate."

Anger flared in my chest, so hot I wouldn't have been surprised to see a puff of smoke come out of my nostrils. "And if I told you that about Ava, what would you have done?"

His brows dropped, but he didn't have a retort. "I get it, but she's going to have to come to Silver Lake eventually."

Not until the baby was born. According to this message, she might not want me in the same state until then. I would miss watching her belly grow round. I'd miss hearing the heartbeat. I'd miss holding her every night, or day, depending on her shift.

I tapped out a quick message. **Can we talk?**

Deacon and I got dressed, then he dropped me off at my pickup.

"Call me later." He was worried about me. He didn't need to be. I wouldn't be doing anything but waiting for some shifter to fuck up so I could clean up the mess.

I drove back to my house. My stomach was growling, but I walked through the place until I stood at the end of my bed, staring down at my duffel bag. If there was a bright side to Avril's message, it was that I didn't have to think about Michael and Darcy. That I wouldn't have to anticipate looking her mom in the eyes when we crossed paths next and feeling like an utter failure that I didn't get there in time.

Deacon had informed the family. Normally a task I took on, but I was grateful for the reprieve. Tonight would suck enough.

I couldn't bring myself to unpack my bag. With a growl, I tossed it onto the floor and kicked it toward the wall.

I was tempted to sit on the end of the bed with my head in my hands and wonder how the hell I could convince Avril to give me a chance while also telling her that days like yesterday and today would continue to happen. Instead, I went to the kitchen. Getting lost in my head after days like this wasn't a good thing. I had learned to keep moving, or I'd get swept under by the tidal wave of emotions.

I took out one of the freezer meals I had prepared for nights like this, when the burden of my position in the clan grew heavy and I didn't feel like following a recipe or watching the clock while I cooked.

It took minutes to heat. I sat at the table to maintain a sense of normalcy. While I ate, I checked my phone at least twenty times. Avril didn't reply to my message.

I changed into a black T-shirt and sweatpants. Next on my to-do list was to mindlessly watch TV. Deacon and Penn sent a couple messages checking in. Thankfully, I changed the sound of their notifications, or I'd have driven myself out of my mind.

A couple hours went by. Nothing but the sound of the TV filled my house. I should be used to it by now, but whenever I noticed the emptiness of the place, it echoed the hollowness inside of me.

I rolled my eyes up to the ceiling and let out a hard breath. A timid knock at the door had me snarling as I got up to answer it.

What the fuck now?

I ripped the door open, uncharacteristically ready to growl at the person on the landing when my gaze collided with Avril's startled brown one.

"Steel, sorry. Is this a bad time?"

I stared at her for several moments, dumbfounded. "Avril?"

"Yes?" she said slowly.

"I thought you never wanted to see me again."

Her brows drew together, and her full lips turned into a frown. "Why would you think that?"

"Your text."

"Right. It was really abrupt. I honestly wasn't sure I would come all the way here. I was afraid I would turn around at the border, and I didn't want to get your hopes up. But I guess I should've been more clear."

I realized I was leaving her standing out in the night with clouds of mosquitos swirling around the streetlights. "Come in, come in. Shit, do you have stuff to bring in?"

"I just have a couple bags—"

I lifted her inside, happy as hell to have my hands on her. "I'll be right back." Snagging the keys from her hand, I took off.

In less than a minute, I had her and her luggage tucked safely into my house.

She was standing in the space between the kitchen and the living room, spinning in a slow circle to take in the house. I went straight to her, wrapped my arms around her, and crushed her to me. My mouth smashed onto hers, but she didn't hesitate to greedily return my kiss.

I had so much to say to her. Words suddenly didn't mean shit when I had her in my arms. I needed to taste her in as many ways as possible.

I walked us to the couch and kneeled in front of it. But before I set her down on the cushions, I yanked her shorts over her ass. A needy moan left her. I wasn't the only one with a one-track mind.

She was here. She was in my fucking home.

"Steel, I need you," she murmured against my lips.

"I'll give you what you need."

She cupped my face with one hand, the fingers of her other digging into my shoulder. "No. Inside me."

The wheels in my brain spun to keep up with what she was asking. She wanted me inside of her. I had thought when that moment came, it'd be nothing but romance. Flowers, chocolate, maybe even a fancy dinner.

I didn't know how I would pull the last part off, but I'd figure it out.

Yet with her taste on my tongue and her sweet peony scent filling my nose, this felt right. It was us. Raw, dirty sex when we both craved the connection.

I yanked her shorts off the rest of the way as she tugged her shirt over her head. Her bra hit the floor next. A quick jerk and my shirt landed next to it. I wouldn't waste time on my pants. I shoved them down and my erection sprang free. Damn, it was almost painful.

We didn't need to worry about protection this time. It had already failed once and made her mine. But I wanted to savor this moment. Treasure entering her when she knew what I really was.

I slowly pushed in. The wet heat of her body clenched around me. I had my hands on her legs, pressing her knees up. Nothing obstructed my view of entering her.

When I was seated to the hilt, I released her legs to palm her breasts and rock back and forth. Her eyes rolled into the back of her head and she groaned. I took my time, stroking in and out, savoring how she felt surrounding every inch of me.

"You're mine," I growled. Desire flared in her eyes. She liked it when I claimed her. Soon, I would tell her what I needed to do to fully claim her. Everyone would know she was mine.

But that was for another time. This was about reconnecting. This was about deepening what was between us. Establishing a real relationship.

Because she had come to Silver Lake. Instead of assuming the worst of me, she had hunted me down and even apologized for thinking she disturbed me.

There was something between us, and I wouldn't give

up on it. And I would make sure she wouldn't give up on me.

Her hands were gripping my shoulders, and she moved her heels to prod my ass cheeks. She'd needed this as badly as me.

"I hope you got enough rest," I grunted. "I plan to fuck you all night."

"Promise?"

I thrust extra hard and her mouth dropped open as she arched her back. "Steel."

"Say it again, baby. I love it when you scream my name while I'm buried inside of you." I dropped my thumb to work her clit. Her body clenched, and she shouted my name.

Pure satisfaction strummed inside my chest. I had been more beast than man for the last twenty-four hours, and hearing her scream my name satisfied my dragon as much as it did me.

I drove into her over and over, resting my thumb on her clit, until she bowed off the couch with my name once again ripping from her lips.

When she hit the peak of her explosion, I gave one more hard thrust and came with a roar.

This was the first time we hadn't used protection. Her demanding body milked my release, and her cries turned incoherent as her climax was magnified.

My hands were clamped on her thighs as I rode out my orgasm. I was locked tight, weathering my own storm as she was experiencing her world being blown apart, but we were in it together.

When we started coming down from our peak, I gathered her in my arms and stretched us both out on the couch. I gave her the inside, letting my ass hang off the edge.

She tucked her head into my chest and draped a leg over my hip. I could take her again, but I let her catch her breath. Questions I should've asked before I attacked her flooded my mind. Instead of dwelling on them, I went ahead and asked. "Why did you come? Don't get me wrong, I'm thrilled you're here. But I thought I messed up so bad you never wanted to see me again—until you had to."

She turned her face to the side, keeping her cheek pressed to the bare skin of my chest. "I called Ava. She told me what you were doing, but she couldn't tell me if you were still alive. I didn't want anything to happen to you, and I missed you. I missed you a lot."

"I didn't mean to worry you." I brushed the backs of my fingers down her cheek. Her big brown eyes were expressive in a way they hadn't been since she'd gotten pregnant. "It all happened so fast. I didn't have my phone with me. Dragons don't have pockets."

She let out a small laugh. "It's a different world you live in, Steel. And I know I have issues with how closely this parallels my mom's life, but what you do in Silver Lake is nothing like what my dad left us for. He left us to help himself, not other people."

I slipped her hand into mine and kissed the back of her fingers. "You don't know this yet, but you are my highest priority. In my job, everything I do for the clan and Deacon is because it'll provide the best life for you and our child."

Her gaze caressed my face. "God, I still can't believe you're real."

"Believe it. I'll spend the rest of my life proving it to you."

She pressed a kiss to my chest, but it was my cock that twitched. "Um… what we just did? Why didn't it feel like that before?"

I couldn't help my wolfish grin. "Our cum enhances the climax. It's one of the traits my kind refused to negotiate when they agreed to blend with the humans."

"I don't know what your ancestors had to give up, but is it selfish to say I'm glad it wasn't that?"

I slid my hand down her body to squeeze her ass. "Want to feel it again?"

∼

AVRIL

IT WAS MORNING, and Steel was sitting with his pants down to his knees in his kitchen chair while I straddled his lap and rode him. This was our third round of sex since I had arrived, but I was still fresh from the fear that I had lost him.

After our second sex session, we'd moved to his bed, and we'd talked. He told me about Michael and Darcy. About how Darcy's mom was still alive, and he never knew what to say after the family was informed. It was my turn to hold him while he discussed the shitty aspects of his work. Then we'd fallen asleep together.

I hadn't thought we'd do it again before he left for work, but our half-eaten breakfast sandwiches were next to us on the table.

I clenched my thighs, rising up and down. His hungry

gaze hardly left my neck, but his hands were all over me, squeezing my ass, kneading my breasts, thrumming my clit.

"Steel, I'm close." As if I had to tell him. I used to need some preparation before sex, but by the time Steel freed his erection, I was dripping.

"You're mine, Avril." The way he growled my name during sex was the most erotic sound I'd ever heard.

I lost it. He wrapped his arms around me and I hugged his head to my chest, his face smashed between my breasts as I moaned and cried incoherent versions of yes. I didn't know sex could be like this. And it wasn't just his magic ejaculate. Everything up to that point was magnified. It was more, and it was because of Steel.

When he moved inside me, it was as if his body fit mine in the way no one else's could. And when I hit my peak, it was higher than I could've imagined. More powerful. More intense. And more... orgasmic.

The fall from the peak was just as blissful. He held me. I had my arms around him. We were connected.

"You're mine," he whispered.

"You like saying that," I murmured with my nose buried in his hair. He said he'd washed in the lake last night, but he smelled like burnt oak, a warm woodsy scent that was strong but comforting. Just like Steel.

"Avril." He tipped his head back to catch my gaze. "I've wanted you since I opened the door to a pissed-off brunette ready to take on a houseful of strange males to save her friend."

If he wasn't still inside me, I would've crawled right back onto him. "I thought I annoyed you."

"It annoyed me I couldn't have you."

I tilted my head and traced his lower lip with my thumb. "Why didn't you try to poach me?"

"You being human added a few levels of complication. And you didn't seem interested."

I had stuffed any infatuation down deep. "I couldn't let myself be interested. It was easier to be irritated with you, even if it was about nothing."

He chuckled and rose, holding me to him. He wrapped one arm around me and used the other to keep his pants from falling down far enough to trip him.

"Where are you going?"

His grin was full of promise. "I think I can be late for work today."

CHAPTER

TEN

S teel

"THAT'S NOT the Steel I said goodbye to yesterday." Deacon's stunned gaze tracked me through his office to where I dropped into the chair I usually sat in.

"It's a different Steel." A sated Steel. For now. Although I would always be ready to take Avril again. "Avril's in town."

His eyes widened. "Really? Ava didn't say anything."

If my expression was smug, it was because I hadn't given Avril much of a chance to do anything, and she had liked it.

Deacon's brow ticked up. "I thought she was going to stay in the city until the baby was born."

"So did I. But when Ava told her what was going on, she got scared, and I guess it helped her make the decision faster than normal. She put in her notice at work."

He sat forward and studied me as if he thought I was joking. "Just like that?"

My good mood took a dip. Why was it so unbelievable? "It's been more than a couple months in the making."

"It hasn't, and you know it."

I would grudgingly give my brother that one. Hadn't I been moping in his office yesterday? And then so dejected when I thought her message was telling me to leave her alone? So, yeah, I could see why Deacon was worried her mind had changed so quickly.

"It was inevitable. We haven't talked a lot about her decision."

"I'm just wondering about what it means if she has doubts and decides to go back. I'm worried for you. There're six months yet before the baby's born."

"I'm aware." I wanted to quit talking about this. I'd come to his office with happy news to share, and he was being a damn downer. "I'll make sure she doesn't have doubts."

"Sorry." He held his hands up like I'd asked him to surrender all his worries. "It's my job to try to spot potential conflict in the clan, but you're my brother. I have faith in you."

He didn't have faith in Avril, but if he was willing to drop the topic, so was I. "Any clan business I need to know about?"

He leaned back in his chair. "Brighton's keeping me updated on the situation in Garnet River, but if you're going back to Minneapolis, can you stop and talk to her?"

"You don't trust she's telling you everything?" Brighton Garnet had come a long way, but secrecy had lined Garnet River's lifestyle for years, long before her family died in a car accident. Shifter clans liked their solitude and flexing control when possible.

"No. It's been two months since she was attacked, but Camden Miller is still at large. He would have healed by now, and he's probably pissed as hell and half-insane after his family was terminated in one night. He's going to be planning."

"I'll go talk to her, maybe explore the area a little, but we have to let nature take its course." Camden Miller and his family had attacked Brighton and Venus when they'd been training together in the woods. My brothers and I found evidence he was also behind the attack on me and Penn, and since he used guns instead of fighting the old way, he had signed his own death warrant.

But Brighton had sworn to kill him. He was hers to deal with, and in our world, if she wasn't strong enough to carry out her job, then she wasn't strong enough to lead. Deacon and I could flush him out like we did with Michael. Penn would help Venus and her brothers. But Garnet River needed to see Brighton handle that specific problem. She had to prove her worth.

"I want her to deal with him, don't get me wrong." Deacon's expression turned pensive. "I can't say I'm not worried though."

"She doesn't have any siblings to support her like you and Lachlan." The sister who would've led the clan had been killed with their parents.

"It wouldn't be a bad thing to remind the clan that she has the support of the Silvers behind her."

I nodded and tapped my fingers on my thighs. After what happened with the domestic, Silver Lake would be pretty quiet today. The town was still shocked and in mourning over the death of two of their own. Reminders that we weren't the immortal beasts we used to be were never easy to handle. Our kind might be able to recover from many illnesses and injuries, but our mental health was exempt.

Still, I should be out there. Let the town see life continued no matter what. "Anything else?"

"Nothing else. Eager to get back to your mate?"

I nodded. Why bother to hide it? She wasn't my mate yet, but after last night, I was hopeful.

"Get out of here then. And I better not catch you working late while she's in town."

"I'll call you before I head back to Minneapolis with her when she works again. She had to put in a month's notice."

He didn't point out that Avril wasn't willing to walk away from her job whenever she wanted. The month's notice was a systemwide requirement for her workplace. If she wanted to work there again, she had to leave in good standing. And, yeah, I wondered why she was concerned about it, but I wouldn't press the subject. Her life was the one drastically changing, and if all she wanted was one more month in Minneapolis, then I wouldn't be an ass about it.

Things were moving fast for her, and the second I forgot that would be when it all fell apart.

AVRIL

I WANDERED through Steel's house. It was a cute little farm-style place on the edge of town. The backyard opened into trees, and I would bet that if I walked one of the trails through them, I'd end at Silver Lake. Ava had said the big lake was on Deacon's land. Family land. Steel didn't act like he had any ownership over the town of Silver Lake, but he took his role of guardian seriously. It made sense he would want to be on the edge of both his family land and the town.

The place had been recently updated. The hardwood floors were darker wood that was more in trend now than when the house was built. Neat trim and crown molding gave every room a shot of character. Steel's bedroom was the largest, but a little smaller than my bedroom. The bathroom was in the hallway, not attached. There was a cute little office right next door. A small square room that made it easy to picture a crib against one wall and a rocking chair in the corner.

I backed out of the office and found another bedroom at the end of the hall. A simple guest room, done in the same style as the rest of the house—warm earth tones that let the bones do the talking.

I found a narrow stairwell across from the guest bedroom. Light streamed from the room it opened into.

My jaw dropped when I crested the last stair. The ceiling met in a peak three feet above my head and angled down on either side to make an A-frame for the room. Built-in bookshelves lined the walls and led to a window seat built into the window.

The bookshelves contained a variety. Children's books. The *Harry Potter* series. A whole set of *Game of Thrones*. Steel had a little bit of everything, like he took a favorite series of each time period of his life and nestled them on the shelves.

But I couldn't picture his large body sprawled in the

window seat. Who was this room for? Did he have an ex who used to like to curl up in the window and read?

Did it matter? He was stuck with me now.

On that sour note, I went downstairs. In the kitchen was a door leading to a flight of stairs down, but all I found in the basement were the utility room, the laundry room, and a storage space. The basement was as cared for as the rest of the place, but not as updated. It was useful, more how I had expected Steel's home to look. The main level was where he lived. In the upper level... I didn't know what that represented.

When I returned to the kitchen, I sat at the table and called Ava. "I'm in town."

"Deacon just called me. Is everything okay?"

My body's answering hum said everything was more than okay. "It's fine. I'm fine. I answered some hard questions I'd been ignoring."

"You really like Steel."

I kicked my feet up on his kitchen chair. Even those were cute and went with the style of the rest of the house. "I really like him." He was handsome with his strong features and that arrogant tilt to his lips. He was a good cook, and he was excellent in bed.

His looks and sex appeal were the easiest to protect myself against, oddly enough. It was the way he watched me eat food he prepared, like a caveman who wanted to beat his chest. Or the way his duty weighed heavily on his shoulders and how hard the responsibility affected him.

When he'd opened the door last night, he'd looked completely thrashed by what he'd had to do. The dejection was there from when he thought I had told him I wanted nothing to do with them. But underneath all that was a man who weathered life alone and was tired of it, but he wouldn't quit. The people in his life meant too much to him.

I wanted to be one of those people. Not by default. He hadn't made me feel that way, so why did my mind keep insisting I was a leech?

Mommy issues, or daddy issues. I could take my pick.

"Are you free for lunch today?" Ava asked.

"Most definitely." There was nothing for me to do in Silver Lake. My future loomed in front of me, wide and empty. I had a month left of work, and I had to move. But beyond that, what was there for me to do?

It was my first day in town. Other than when I had been here with Ava, and I had stayed with her at Deacon's place. Venus had taken us driving around, but I had been a tourist.

Silver Lake was going to be my home. And I was going to have to face it sooner or later.

Ava gave me directions to the little diner on Main Street, not that I wouldn't be able to find it on my own.

I finished getting ready and hopped into my car.

People going about their day stopped to study me and my car as I drove past. Not many strangers came through town. According to Steel, the residents were all members of the clan. Wildrose wasn't far away, and had more of a mixture of humans and shifters, but it was more of a crossroads than Silver Lake. Very few people were driving through. And everyone staring at me knew I was here for a reason.

Parking at the diner, I took a deep breath. Ava's car was here, so I was safe to go in. I got out. Prickles of awareness danced across my skin. They weren't the tingly kind, like when Steel was looking at me. As I walked to the diner, they centered between my shoulder blades. I was the stranger in town. If this was how it felt before anyone learned about me and him, what would it be like after?

The scents of grease and grilled burgers hit my nose. My appetite roared despite the big breakfast Steel had made me.

Ava grinned and waved. Her golden hair was in a high ponytail and her skin glowed more radiant than ever. Regular sex with a partner who wasn't a dick looked good on her.

She jumped out of the booth and encompassed me in a giant bear hug. "It feels like forever since I've seen you, and I know it's only been a couple of months."

I hugged her in return, harder than I intended. It had only been two months, but it seemed more like two years. We used to get together regularly, and then she had moved. I missed being around my best friend.

When we were seated at a booth, an older woman—a shifter?—appeared at our sides. "What can I get you?" Her nostrils flared, and she peered at me.

Ava's gaze darted from her to me, and she ran her lower lip between her teeth. Apparently, there was something I needed to know. Did I smell?

Was it another shifter thing I didn't understand?

"I'll have the everything omelet and hash browns please. Can you add a couple extra eggs too?" Was that a weird request? I had never asked for extra eggs in my omelet.

"Sure thing," she answered lightly but kept a brow lifted.

Her expression reminded me of going to the downtown diner when I was growing up. The waitresses had that look when taking Mom's order. Like they knew about her and didn't approve. I pushed the menu to the side.

Ava ordered a burger and fries. When the server disappeared, I leaned forward. "Do I smell?"

Her smile was understanding. "Not in the way you think. It could be because you're an unknown human. I'm not sure if she can tell you're pregnant, or if she can smell Steel all over you."

My cheeks flamed hot. People in town could tell I'd had sex recently—and with who? "Is it a close proximity thing? Is that how they can tell I've been with Steel?"

She shook her head, regret in her eyes. "No. I mean, maybe there's some of that."

I slumped in the booth and blew out a breath. The lady's expression said she knew who I had sex with and didn't approve. "That's messed up."

"If it helps at all, I know. I'm still going through it."

I leaned forward and whispered, "Do you think they can tell I'm pregnant?" Anxiety robbed some of my appetite. I didn't want to be the stranger sleeping with one of their bachelors and oops, look, I was having his kid.

She lifted a shoulder. "I don't know. We'll have to ask Venus."

I rubbed my temples. "I feel like everyone's watching me."

Her gaze swept the diner. Only a few other people were dining and the door chimed with new arrivals. She didn't deny that I was getting looks.

I couldn't stand getting looks.

My chest tightened. I hadn't hyperventilated before, but my quick breaths were getting close. "I hate this."

Sympathy filled her gaze, and I was transported back

to high school. Ava had been my anchor in the storm of my life. She had been the steady presence, the one who knew what was happening and stayed with me regardless. She didn't care how I was raised or what people said. She was my ride or die.

I didn't want to go back to those years. I had come so far.

"You have every right to be here." She covered my hand with hers, and it was enough to yank my brain out of the memories. "Breathe in. Breathe out."

I gazed into her teal eyes and slowed my heart rate. I wasn't a kid. I was an adult and my relationship with Steel was no one's business.

Okay, it was some people's business with the shifter thing, but no one in this diner had the right to interfere. What if they did? For some reason, the thought calmed me. This was nothing like when I was growing up. The way I was treated was the fault of others. Not me. What happened between me and Steel had factors I couldn't have imagined when I was younger. None of it was my fault. I had changed my life for issues that hadn't been about me; they'd only involved me without my permission.

I had traveled far away from home and put down roots. But I lived my life like I was still avoiding people. When I was at my job, I was treated like a hero—unless I had a cranky patient. Then I was treated like crap. But a patient's poor treatment had nothing to do with how I was raised, and I'd convinced myself that was different. I'd spent my life running from the same treatment I dove right into at the hospital.

I had to think about that.

"You have to let me know when you need help

moving." Ava's gaze darted around the café again. She was nervous on my behalf. How many meals like this had she endured because I'd handed power over to others?

"I haven't figured out the time line yet, but I appreciate it."

The food arrived. I ate with a little more restraint than I would've used at my place or Steel's, and I refused to be hyperaware of people around me. I noticed them like they had noticed me.

After I was scrutinized as the newbie in town, everyone minded their own business. Older guys that looked like they came to town to meet for lunch sat at the counter. Couples laughed comfortably together in other booths. And in the corner was a family with small kids.

Were they shifters? The two boys each colored a sheet of paper, but it was like they had a case of the wiggles. They couldn't sit still. I didn't think that was odd, except there was a force to their movements as they bumped into each other. Like they had to get energy out somehow otherwise they would combust. A baby whacked her spoon against the high chair, creating a cacophony that should irritate patrons. No one paid them any attention.

This was normal behavior. If I was at a restaurant in the city, this family would be getting shot glares from most customers in the place. Steel said our child would have to go to a special shifter school. If this was only a hint of the reason, accepting my fate might be easier.

No matter what, I wanted what was best for the baby.

Ava must've noticed much of my tension had drained and she dug into her meal. I was done eating before her and pushed my plate away to watch out the window. A bakery was across the street with a sign that said Miss Mabel's.

Ava caught the direction of my gaze. "It's an excellent bakery. It's like Steel's second home." A curl of jealousy rose, but Ava shook her head. "Miss Mabel opened the place when she was in her twenties. The name stuck."

So no young, single baker was Steel's unrequited love. Next to the bakery was a small, narrow building, barely reaching two stories stuffed between the older, larger brick structures next to it. The faded sign was of a stork holding a basket with a blanket spilling out. "What's that place?"

"I don't know that it has a name. Mathilda is Miss Mabel's mate and the local midwife. She's a little younger than Miss Mabel, but she's still the practicing midwife in the area."

"A midwife? Like officially?"

"Officially?"

"Like, Deacon's the mayor, but..."

Her mouth formed an O. "I don't know. Want to go ask her?"

I shook my head. "No, it's just that she'd have to be a nurse first in this state. Then get her master's degree and certification. It's a process. But I didn't know if she'd have to do that here."

"Everything's as official as it can get."

I stared at the little business, curiosity brewing in my chest. I knew nothing about what her job entailed other than what I had learned in school. Questions flowed through my head in a steady stream. She was a mate, but was she human or shifter?

She was likely a shifter, but she'd been able to carve a healthcare niche for herself in a tiny shifter town.

It got me thinking. Perhaps it was time to carve my place somewhere. To fit myself in instead of hiding.

Ava polished off her last fry. "Do you want to go back to my place?"

I was okay in the diner. Surprisingly at ease when everyone could sniff out who I'd been with and what we'd been doing. But I also looked forward to talking to my friend when we weren't lamenting over the crappy guys in our life. "Yes, can we invite Venus?"

She grinned. "Already did. She had a couple of clients to finish first and then she'll be over."

We left the diner, and I got into my car to follow her back to her place. My phone pinged. A message from Steel. **Everything all right?**

Yeah, why?

I stopped at home for lunch.

Right. And I was gone. I wasn't used to checking in, not with my mom, and Ian hadn't cared what I was doing until he needed something. Steel wasn't demanding constant updates, but I wasn't used to someone worrying about me. Had he thought I left him again?

Just in case he was worried, I sent, **I met Ava for lunch and now I'm going to her place.**

Have fun.

I made a mental note to get better at communication. We'd been talking through some deep topics and I forgot the minor ones were important too. I wanted this to work. I wanted his feeling for me to be real. I wanted... to find out if this life was one I could be happy in. Could I thrive instead of hide?

I gave the stork sign one last look before I pulled away.

CHAPTER

ELEVEN

S teel

THE LAST THREE days had been a dream come true. I went to work. Came home to my future mate. Made love all evening, and woke up with her in my arms. But she still had a month left to work, and business to attend to in Minnesota so she could move to Silver Lake.

I was just outside of Garnet River. Avril had taken her car back and was probably already at home. I wanted to get the Garnet River business out of the way so I could dedicate my time to my mate.

Despite the bliss of the last three days, she had grown quiet and didn't leave the house. When I asked her what was wrong, she'd just shrugged and said she had a lot on her mind. I sensed no lie, but I had hoped she'd open up about it. Was it arranging the movers? Selling her condo? Did she hate Silver Lake more than she thought?

Perhaps while she was in her own place, she would talk. Her safety and the safety of our child was of the utmost importance to me, but almost as critical was her happiness. I didn't think she realized how much she meant to me.

I'd keep trying to prove it.

I pulled into Garnet River and parked in front of city hall. Some improvements had begun since I'd been here last. The rubble from the most decrepit buildings was getting cleaned up. Large metal bins for trash and a dump truck lined the sidewalk. Now that the hoard belonging to Brighton's family had been found, she could use it to improve her clan. The worth of the gems might not have reached the millions, but it was enough to help them help themselves, which was more than they had before.

Brighton Garnet was expecting me. Selma from the council met me at the entrance.

Her warm smile deepened the wrinkles on her face. "Thank you so much for coming, Steel. It means a lot to Garnet to have the support of the Silvers."

After Penn and I had been attacked, and we learned how poorly Garnet clan was functioning, Deacon nearly enacted Silver law. He would've been in charge of the clan in Garnet River. But with Venus's help, we had learned what the root of the problem was, and now Garnet River could thrive.

But like Deacon had said, the clan wasn't out of the woods yet. With that Miller male still at large, Brighton's life was in danger, and she could get challenged by any other member of Garnet River. So, yeah, showing up here was in all our best interests. Because Brighton wasn't interested in power beyond how she could give her people their best life. That was one of the most important qualities of a leader.

I followed Selma into the main meeting area of city hall. The room used to be the old dining room of the bar. Brighton sat at a small, round table. An empty chair was across from her. She had one long leg crossed over the other, and although confidence filled her gaze that hadn't been there the first time I met her, nervous energy vibrated off her.

She gave Selma a quick smile. "Thank you." She rose to greet me, shaking my hand with a solid grip. "How are you, Steel?"

I was ten years older than this girl, but I admired her spirit. She had a *fake it 'til you make it* attitude, and she would continue to grow into a fine leader. "I am well. I was going to be in the area anyway, and Deacon wanted me to stop by."

Her smile turned understanding. "A little show of power for those who still oppose me?"

I lifted a shoulder. "Figured it couldn't hurt. Is there anything you require of the Silvers?"

Her mouth tightened briefly, but she shook her head. "No, nothing I can pinpoint. I'm more interested in seeing how things change after your visit."

"What do you mean?"

"It's more of a feeling." She fell quiet for several moments, but I didn't push her. If she was telling me, it was significant. And since she was so young, and fairly new to her position, I would give her the benefit of time. Something we didn't always have. "I think I'm being watched."

I nodded. She probably was, and she would know that. "How is this different?"

"I haven't determined whether Camden has connections and spies within city limits, but I would be foolish to rule it out. I assume my movements and my daily activities are being tracked, but…" Her gaze swept the room as if she was double-checking that everyone had indeed left. "I would also be foolish if I assumed Camden was my only enemy."

So, not just Camden and those who supported him, but another party who would gladly destroy one or both of them. Interesting. "Any idea who?"

"No, but changes are coming. Not just the normal ones of trying to improve the town." Sadness darkened the red in her eyes, but she blinked it away. "Selma's getting older. She's tired. Not only was she my guardian for several years, but I value her as a council member. She hasn't said she wants to retire, but she's ready. She didn't recover from that night as well as we had hoped."

That night. The night Camden and his family attacked her and Venus. Selma and the rest of Garnet River's council had joined my brothers and me to hunt for them, crashing her dragon through the trees.

"Is there a good candidate to take her place?"

Brighton shook her head. "Not someone I could trust like her." She huffed. "Not someone I could trust half as much as her."

A dragon shifter was the strongest when they had two things—a family to watch their backs, and a strong and knowledgeable council to advise them. Brighton's family had been killed, and there was a good possibility she would lose ground with her council without Selma. Shifter rulers were born, but the council members were voted in. If Camden had generated enough doubt in a good number of townsfolk, the results of the vote would not be in Brighton's favor.

I thought for a moment, hating the idea that was blossoming. But we were dragon shifters, and what might sound appalling to a human was good practice to a shifter. "Remember the deal you wanted to strike with Penn?"

Her gaze grew wary, and she brushed her gaze over my body as if she thought I was an adequate cut of beef but she'd rather pick from another menu. "I thought you were in Minnesota for a human female."

Deacon would've told her why I was in the state so she didn't think my trip was solely to check on her. "Not me." Relief passed through her gaze. "I will be mating Avril, yes."

Brighton's expression softened, like she was grateful to hear good news no matter who it came from. "Congratulations."

I could've puffed my chest out with pride, but I still had my work to do in that regard. "You don't have family," I said gently. "And if you don't have a strong council, it's going to be hard to continue the path you're on without their support."

She dipped her head. "The only question is who?" Her tone was rigid, her words stilted.

Empathy for her nestled in my chest. She had proposed a mating contract between her and Penn even though she had just met my brother. She'd fought for her position but was still faced with having to find a mate instead of discovering love on her own.

I racked my brain for ideas. It would need to be a power play. Anyone from the Silver clan was out. Deacon and Penn were mated, and I soon would be too. "Is there anyone you're, you know…"

"Seeing?" She shook her head, and her gaze skittered away. Talking with a guy who was barely a friend about this had to be unnerving. "Camden would've been the best option if he hadn't been a power-hungry asshole. And just a douche in general."

I knew the ruling families in the other clans. There were single males in line for ruler but had siblings who attained the position. The problem was I didn't know what they were like morally. The clan Silver had become the closest to was, oddly enough, Jade.

For generations, Jade clan had opposed authority as much as possible without causing an all-out war. They'd done as much as they could do to keep from signing their own death decree. But under Lachlan, the clan had stabilized and their aggression with it.

Lachlan was mated. Venus was with my brother. That left Ronan. I didn't know a lot about him either, but he might be worth considering.

"Ronan Jade."

Brighton's eyes flared. "I don't—we can't possibly—not Ronan."

Curiosity got the better of me. Ronan had come to help save Venus that night. He'd stayed for a few days while his sister healed. Venus had stayed a few extra days to mate Penn just shy of her thirty-fifth birthday. Brighton knew Ronan. So it didn't bode well that she was so against it.

The answer seemed too good to be true, but if one or the other was against it, then I hated to force it. "Why not Ronan?"

Pink bloomed in her cheeks, and she rose. She shoved

her chair in and paced the room, an arm across her belly and her other hand flying as she spoke. "He's crass, for one. He thinks he knows everything. He's got that Jade attitude. You know, the one that rebels against authority?" She spun to face me. "Can you imagine what he'd be like mated to me? I'm the ruler. It would eat at him."

"But he's used to working for his brother."

"His brother doesn't have boobs."

"Venus does." I didn't want to minimize her worry, but I had to understand if her most valid reason for not mating Ronan was a personality conflict. "She's older than him. He's the youngest of the Jade ruling family. Do you really think he'd have trouble letting you continue in your position?"

"I think he'll have a problem keeping his mouth shut and not pissing me off."

Personality conflict it was. Except the more I thought about the union, the more it made sense. Jade clan was pulling itself up from the rubble Lachlan, Venus, and Ronan's parents had left behind. They knew how to take a clan that had been ground down to almost nothing and create a strong foundation. Brighton could use that expertise.

"Jade has been doing really well for itself. They're growing. The clan respects Lachlan, and he's getting them involved in investments and gentrification. Ronan's been with his brother through all of it. He could have a lot of insight."

She flattened her mouth and continued pacing. "That male can't possibly commit. I won't be made to look like a fool by my partner."

I didn't want that for her either. And I wasn't sure if that was a risk with Ronan. But the idea was worth following up on. "Ultimately, you're going to have the final say. But I'll discuss the idea with Deacon, and he can approach Lachlan. Deacon won't follow through if Lachlan thinks Ronan can't help you."

"I don't want Ronan's help."

She'd made that obvious. But shifters didn't have dating apps. She was tied to Garnet River during all her free time. Leading the clan and remodeling the town so it stayed inhabitable were her full-time job and her hobby for the foreseeable future. "If you can, meet someone else. Otherwise, you have to admit it's a good pairing. Just something to think about."

She tossed a frustrated glance my way while she paced. Her expression told me changing her mind would be a challenge only Ronan could achieve, and I wasn't sure if he would want to. She lifted her chin and squared her shoulders as if shedding the topic by letting it roll off her back. "Your future mate. She's human too, right?"

Brighton had met Ava during Venus and Penn's mating ceremony. But she would've heard about Avril during her time with Venus. "Yes."

"I want to officially extend an invitation to you both. You're welcome here anytime." Her gaze strayed toward the front of the building. "The people in this town need to realize that there's a lot of mate potential out there. The Millers poisoned their thinking about taking human mates as a way of control. We need to get out there and meet new people. But at the same time, I don't want the fallout of shifters behaving badly around humans. Still, it would be good for them to see more shifter-human pairings."

I would love to take her up on the offer, but I had

Avril's safety to consider. "How hostile are your shifters toward humans?"

She chewed her lower lip as she pondered. "I heard no grumblings about Ava, but it's possible they just didn't reach me."

When Ava had been here, so had my brothers and me, and Venus and her brothers. No one from Garnet clan would've dared say a word against Ava.

Would it be the same for Avril? "I'll talk to her about it."

Avril had to get to know my world, and I couldn't make all the decisions for her.

Brighton smiled wistfully. I sensed she would like to have a chance to make another friend. She had gotten close with Venus and had latched onto Ava during the ceremony. And it would be good for Avril to know another person in the shifter world. A ruler, no less.

I said my goodbyes and went back out to my pickup. It was time to return to my mate.

AVRIL

STACKING a box full of college textbooks onto another box filled with the books I saved from growing up, I looked around the basement. Steel was loading all the books in my to-be-read pile into a different box. I had almost told him to leave those out. I'd had them for years, but perhaps I'd have time to get to them in Silver Lake.

I could picture them in that cute little reading room, on the shelves next to Steel's books.

Ian used to bug me when I was trying to read. I had joked it was a good thing I met him after I was finished with most of my college, otherwise I wouldn't have graduated. I didn't think it was a joke. Studying and reading took my focus off him, and he'd pestered me until it was easier to put the book down and do something with him.

An image of my mom flashed in my head. She would sit in the recliner, facing out the big picture window, her gaze distant and a forgotten book dropping out of her hand. I thought she'd been waiting for my dad to return.

I suppressed a shudder. That wouldn't be me. It couldn't.

I kept thinking about the midwife. I didn't meet her while I was in Silver Lake. I hadn't gone out after my day with Ava. When Steel worked, I snuggled into the reading nook and reacquainted myself with some favorite books from my childhood. When I hadn't been reading, I'd been staring out the window—not like my mother. But I'd thought about Mathilda. Could she use an assistant?

I'd been too afraid to ask. Too scared I'd get rejected. And then what?

Steel closed the box and glanced at me as if he sensed something was wrong. He didn't ask, just waited for me to talk.

Ian had never been able to tell when something was bothering me. Steel was the exact opposite. But he didn't bug me. He didn't pry. He waited for me to be ready to talk to him.

Determined to communicate better, I admitted what was on my mind. Mostly. "I'm just wondering what I'm going to do in Silver Lake."

"Anything you want."

"Except be a nurse."

He straightened. "Wildrose isn't far away. They have a clinic. Some Silver shifters are allowed to live there because it's so close to Silver Lake, and it helps them get out to meet new people. It's nothing like the big hospitals around here, but maybe they have an opening."

"Not many employers want to hire someone who's expecting and will be gone for maternity leave, and then might have to take a bunch of sick days for her kid."

He abandoned his packing and crossed to me. "Of all the career fields, I would think the medical field would understand."

I snorted. "Sometimes they're the worst."

He gathered me in a hug, as if he sensed it wasn't the job I was concerned about as much as how I couldn't end up like my mom.

I buried my face in his broad, warm chest. Inhaled his singed-oak scent.

"It'll be all right," he murmured.

I needed to hear it. I'd had Ava next to me most of my life, telling me everything would be fine. Building me up when everyone stomped me down. Then I let myself get swindled by a guy. The Avril I'd worked so hard to construct had been getting dismantled without me noticing.

But Steel wasn't like that. He brought back what I had been missing in my life.

"You're going to have me." He rubbed his hands up and down my back. "For those sick days. It's not all going to fall on you. I'm going to be there too."

I squeezed my eyes shut. How could I keep forgetting? I would have a partner. After going through my life mostly alone, I couldn't blame myself for having trouble accepting the idea of a partner.

He stroked my hair. "Did something new bring these worries up, or is it the actual moving?"

I pushed back from him and licked my dry lips. "The moving. It's bringing back memories."

He wrapped his big hand around mine and led me to the guest room bed. If he wanted to distract me with sex, I was up for it. It was better than the spinning wheels in my head.

But he sat down and tugged me down next to him. "About your mom?"

When did it become *not* about my mom? Was there a point where I was using her as an excuse to stay in a place that wasn't right for me just because it was different from what I had known?

I didn't have the answer. "I told you a little bit about what it was like growing up. My mom never said she got pregnant on purpose, but I wouldn't be surprised if she did. My grandparents pressured my dad to marry her, even though he wanted to go to college out of state. But he married her, had me, and they just existed. I don't remember much—he left when I was pretty little. But I remember playing by myself in my bedroom while Mom sat in her chair and waited for him to come home."

"Did you know she was waiting for him?"

I was about to say yes when I stopped. How had I known she was waiting for him? I had assumed she was. It was better when Dad was home, but that was because he talked to me and played with me. When he was around, Mom came to life.

But what if she hadn't been sitting there waiting for him? "What else would she have been doing?" I wasn't asking Steel for the answer. I wasn't sure who could answer that. Other than her.

"I can't say I know much about human women."

The corner of my mouth lifted at his answer, but I didn't take my stare off the wall. What had been going through Mom's mind? "When Dad left, she started drinking. I guess she drank before that." Frowning, I pictured the trailer house I was raised in. A can of beer was always on the end table, but before Dad got home, it would be gone. "She was a closet drinker." Why hadn't I tried to understand Mom earlier? I twisted sideways and put my hand on Steel's arm. "She was fighting her addiction from the beginning. When Dad was around, it was at a simmer. And when he left, he gave her the perfect excuse to overindulge. And then she went looking for love in all the wrong places."

"It must've been hard for you."

Hard wasn't the word I'd use. Isolating. Lonely. Frustrating. "I used to sit in that chair like she did. Waiting for her to come home. Until eventually, I decided I didn't want to be like her."

"She didn't have anyone?"

His question made all the blood in my veins crystallize, creeping along, forming tiny icicles. "I mean, she had..." The other men. Mom had been depressed and lonely, and she sought comfort with anyone who would give it to her. And I had hated her for it. I hadn't understood, I didn't try to understand, and I hated her.

I wasn't ready to say those words out loud, to admit how wrong I might've been. Mom could've had a thousand best friends at all the bars she went to when she left me alone in the trailer. As soon as I had been old enough to keep child protection services away, she had spent her evenings and nights elsewhere. Her mental status didn't justify her behavior. None of that justified neglecting her child. None of it helped that her actions were taken out on me. It was done.

But… it helped to understand her. Just like kids had teased me instead of having compassion for my situation, Mom had been taken advantage of.

"I guess I didn't know much about her, or if she had close friends." I didn't know anything about her now. I hadn't talked to her since I left town. "Ava's parents made sure I was fed and had clean clothes. Ava's mom taught me how to do laundry and housecleaning so I could keep the trailer from becoming a cesspool."

"I'm glad you had them. And you'll still have her. And her father." He tipped my chin up until my gaze met his. "You'll have me. No matter what, you'll have me."

I swiped at the hot tears running down my face. I'd been able to keep these emotions bottled up for the last several years, but damn these pregnancy hormones. "Can we quit packing for a while and fool around?"

His brows lifted. "You want to have sex?"

I nodded and waved my hands up and down my body. "I feel like I'm bursting out of my skin. All these emotions need an outlet."

I thought he'd kiss me, we'd tumble back, and he'd fuck me into oblivion. But the surprise was gone from his expression, leaving concern behind. "I want to bury myself inside you every chance I get, but this seems like something you need to talk about."

"We've already talked."

Doubt entered his eyes and fueled my irritation. "Fine. Might as well finish packing." I jumped up and stomped to the door.

"Avril—"

I held up a hand. "We talked, Steel. I don't know what

else you expect from me." More talking and I'd be a useless puddle on the ground. Nothing but a pool of guilt. My insides were raw.

"I expect to get to know you. I expect to be your partner in bed and out. That includes talking about what's bothering us, and the topic of your mom is bothering you. But you've avoided it for years, and you're angry that I've called you out on it."

How dare he? How dare he be so observant? Why couldn't he be a self-centered jackass like my ex? Like my dad? It would be easier to stay angry at him.

It would be easier to keep blaming someone else for how I felt. Did others have a huge part in making me feel bad? Absolutely. But continuing to let it eat away at me threatened my happiness.

I was having a baby, dammit. And the only difference between me and my mother was a guy who didn't feel trapped with me. Steel liked having sex with me. He wanted to get to know me. He'd said he wasn't good at romance, but he was good at being there for me.

Everything welled up inside me, pushing outward, until hot tears streamed down my cheeks. My shoulders shook, and I realized I was sobbing. Steel was there in a second. I was tucked into his warm embrace and carried to bed. He didn't kiss me or strip me down. He held me, and I cried.

He was my partner. He was here. But he didn't love me and maybe that was what bothered me the most.

CHAPTER

TWELVE

S teel

AVRIL WAS on the first day of her stretch of days off. We had talked about going back to Silver Lake, but she had a lot to do in Minnesota to get ready to move. She'd spent part of the day on the phone with a real estate agent, and then she'd taken pictures to send to the agent for the sale. It was a seller's market, and the place should sell quickly.

After her breakdown, while we were packing, she'd been focused on moving and work. No more discussion about her past. Or our future other than moving.

I sat on the couch with my feet kicked up on the coffee table. Avril's head was in my lap and she was napping. I shut the sound off on my phone, but I watched the screen to track Deacon's messages.

I had told him about my proposal for a mating

contract between Brighton and Ronan. He'd also been filled in with the description of Brighton's reaction.

Both Deacon and Lachlan supported the proposal. Lachlan swore his brother wouldn't be a shitty mate, not after the parents they'd had. Lachlan claimed the only thing Ronan was guilty of was a considerable lack of charm.

So Deacon and I were going back and forth about how we could talk Brighton into agreeing to give the mating serious thought. Lachlan said he'd deal with Ronan.

Venus's name appeared on my phone. She wasn't messaging me, she was calling. I didn't want to wake Avril, so I answered quietly. "Venus."

She lowered her voice to mock mine. "Steel."

I rolled my eyes, but grinned. I'd known Venus my whole life, but now that she was officially my sister, I could get playfully annoyed with her. "I take it you heard about our plan with your brother?"

"Oh, I heard, but not from my brother—or your brothers."

Penn would hear about the last part, and he probably didn't even know. "Brighton told you?"

"Yes, and I know you Silvers well enough to know that you won't let this idea go."

"So you don't think Brighton should mate Ronan?"

"I didn't say that. I am saying that you and Deacon are probably wondering how to convince Brighton. Deacon doesn't want to order her, but neither of you can figure out what else to do."

Spot on. "You think it's a good plan though? She's so damn young, and I don't know your brother."

Avril pushed off my lap, rubbing her eyes. I had talked to her about what my meeting in Garnet River had been about. If she overheard the conversation, that would save me from explaining it again.

"She is really damn young. And my brother can be a stubborn jackass—a lovable one, but that's me saying it. His sibling. It's going to be harder for Brighton to warm to a stubborn jackass when she's been harassed by Camden for the last decade of her life."

That was the crux of the issue. The obstacle we were trying to work around. "He irritated the crap out of her when he was there."

"And he'll irritate the crap out of her if they mate. But... if they get to know each other, things could change."

"They would have their whole lives to get to know each other."

"Not if they are forced together. She's a stubborn one too. No, what we have to do is give Ronan a reason to be in Garnet River. Then nature can take its course."

I was doubtful. Venus had a good intuition about people. Her insight was what saved Garnet River. But she hadn't seen what I had. Brighton had been adamant. "Nature already took its course. Your brother pissed her off."

"He might be an acquired taste. Do you want Deacon to have to order her to mate Ronan? Because their relationship won't go anywhere if he does. Ronan might have a thick shell, but he won't like being forced on a female. And as prideful as Ronan may be, he's going to be offended at her unwillingness to be with him. On Brighton's end, she's going to resent that she was forced to be with him. And every time Ronan opens his mouth, she's going to think he lacks faith in her ability. And she'll be extra prickly because her clan will know that she was ordered to mate. The mating would be in name only, which won't be strong enough for Brighton or Garnet River."

I worked over the points Venus made. They were important, critical even. I wanted the best for Brighton and her clan. But I also wanted her happy. I was seeing how hard it was for Avril to turn away from all the plans she had made and be maneuvered into a life she had actively avoided. So, no. We needed to make this as much of Brighton and Ronan's idea as possible. "Okay, so what's a good reason to put Ronan in Garnet River for a few months?"

"If there's one thing my brother excels at, it's breaking shit down. If something needs demolishing, put him on it. If there is remodeling to be done, stick a paintbrush in his hands. He downplays his remodeling skills. He's self-taught, and he's good. Put him to work."

"But Brighton is going to know what we're doing."

"She'll know. He'll know too. We've planted the idea. The possibility. As long as we don't force it, maybe something can grow."

A soft lick of heat brushed over my face. Avril was watching me. I liked having her in my business. I hadn't enjoyed hiding the real reason Penn and I stayed in Minneapolis so long when we'd been hooking up.

"Thanks, Venus. I'll talk to Deacon if you want to talk to your brother."

"I've already straightened them both out."

My lips twitched. I was sure she had. And Penn had probably laughed the entire time. "So what did you call me for?"

"I'm going to call Brighton, but I think you should be there to greet my brother. Make it look like a multi-clan collaboration. He's stubborn, but can't resist a challenge."

"Got it."

After I hung up with her, I tossed my phone on the coffee table and put my feet on the floor. "Sorry to wake you up."

Avril blinked, trying to wipe the rest of the sleepiness out of her eyes. "It's okay. I want to be able to sleep tonight. So that was Venus?"

"Did you hear what she said?"

Avril shook her head, her brow furrowed as if wondering why I would think she would've heard a word on the other end of the phone. Right. Her human hearing wouldn't have been able to pick up the entire conversation. I summarized the discussion.

"You have to play matchmaker?"

"You're welcome to come with me." I said it before I thought about the consequences. Would she be safe? My gut said yes. Residents of the town might scorn human mates, but they wouldn't do so in front of me. Brighton was the only one in physical danger in Garnet River, and Camden was likely to stay far away if he knew a Steel was within city limits.

"You want me along?"

"Brighton said you're welcome anytime." I had to be completely honest with her. We were in this together and only trouble would come from secrets. "One of the ways Brighton's enemy tried to poison the town against her was to nurture the thought that dragon shifters shouldn't take human mates."

"I thought you said it was common."

"It is. It's necessary too. But it was a way for the Millers to isolate their clan even more."

She nodded, understanding lighting her eyes. "You think they'll say something?"

"They would risk being challenged by me if they did. But if you sense some hostility, that could be why, and we'll leave as soon as you want to. But Brighton would like to show that it's a normal part of our culture, and I think she'd like to get to know you. She doesn't have many friends."

Avril ran her lower lip between her teeth. "How long do I have to think about it?"

"As soon as I hear from Venus when Ronan will be in town. If Deacon wants me there when Ronan arrives, then that's the next time I plan to be in Garnet River."

"Okay. I'll consider it until then."

She had faced some of her feelings toward her mother. Both her old emotions, and the new ones an adult Avril feels. I didn't wish to open up wounds from her past by getting dirty looks in Garnet River, but I didn't want her to feel like I was hiding her from my people. "No pressure either way. Hungry?"

She playfully rolled her eyes. "You know I am."

AVRIL

I COULDN'T BELIEVE I was moving tomorrow. I had worked the rest of my shifts, had my going away party, and my home was packed in boxes and ready for the moving truck arriving in the morning.

I hadn't thought I'd get to see Garnet River, but Ronan had agreed to help with the demolition and renovations of the downtown. He was supposed to arrive today.

Garnet River was smaller than I thought. I could walk from one end of town to the other in just a few minutes. Steel had warned me what it would be like on the way here, and I reined in my gawking. I didn't want to be insulting. Especially to people who could turn into dragons and bite my head off.

Anxiety unfurled in my belly. Silver Lake had been intimidating, but for as small as Garnet River was, it loomed in front of me like a great unknown chasm.

I tried to tell myself that they liked humans just fine, they just didn't want them mating their shifters. But I was coming here as a human, mating a shifter, so that didn't help ease my mind. Even if they didn't know who I was, they would smell the story on me like the diners in Silver Lake.

He pulled in front of a building that looked like an old saloon. City hall. He told me about this place too.

A young woman came out. Her long black braid hung over one shoulder. She aimed a smile at Steel, but it widened when she saw me. The nerves in my stomach settled.

When I got out of the pickup, she greeted me first. "Welcome, Avril. I feel like I know you already from Venus."

Hearing Venus's name prompted a smile. I was going to mate a shifter, and I had a shifter as a close friend. The residents of Garnet River could have issues with me, but it would be their problem, and I was no longer accepting the emotional toll of others' baggage.

"It's nice to meet you, Brighton. Thank you for the invite."

"Ronan's not here yet?" Steel's eyes scanned up and down Main Street. If one of the six cars lining Main Street wasn't Ronan's, I didn't know where else in town he could be parked. Houses were scattered a few blocks on either side of the road, but most of the residents lived rurally.

Brighton's expression darkened, and she glared in the direction we had driven into town from. "He said he would get here when he got here." Her flat tone was unimpressed with Ronan's attitude.

I hadn't met Venus's brothers, but from what little I knew, and after my short time of knowing Brighton, I hoped she made him work for it.

A muscle jumped in Steel's jaw, but he dropped the topic of Ronan. "No worries. We can chat until then. It'll be nice to talk without having it revolve around business."

The yearning in Brighton's eyes told me that she thought the same. In a town this size, she probably didn't have a lot of people her age that she could socialize with, and not in the position she was in.

"Come on over to the house. Ronan was going to stop here, but if he's late, he'll just have to find us."

I liked this girl more and more.

The walk to Brighton's place took only a few minutes. The old farmhouse had been kept up relatively well. Signs of its age could be seen on the recently painted but peeling siding and the bent and dented gutter system. The porch that stretched from end to end appeared sturdy enough, but could use a good sanding and staining.

We followed her to the front door.

She unlocked the door and held it open. "I have some

burgers to grill if you'd like to stay and eat. Selma is a grill master and taught me all of her tricks."

My stomach awakened and made its persistent rumble.

Steel chuckled. "That sounds great, thank you. We would've brought something to contribute to the meal if we knew it was a cookout."

"My treat." Brighton beckoned for us to follow her. The floors creaked in the stereotypical way of old hardwood floors as we walked through a tidy, square living room into an open concept kitchen.

I went with Steel out a squeaky sliding door to a back patio. Brighton came out a few minutes later with the raw burgers on the plate.

We chatted like two women getting to know each other. It was refreshing. I couldn't visit much with my patients, and their family was often focused on the well-being of their loved one, rightfully so. I could chat with my coworkers, but I wasn't close to any of them.

Talking with Brighton was as easy as getting to know Venus had been. Steel went back and forth between the house and the patio, retrieving anything Brighton might need for cooking. Mostly, I thought he wanted to make sure our conversation wasn't interrupted.

The backyard was fenced in, but the place next door looked abandoned. Windows were boarded up, and the lawn was overgrown. There was nothing but an empty lot with overgrown bushes on the other side.

Brighton's backyard was as cared for as the inside of the house. Neatly mowed with trimmed shrubs. I liked this place. It was homey and reminded me of Steel's place. I was glad she invited us to eat here instead of going to the diner across the street from city hall.

I was about to ask if the shrubs on the far end of her yard were lilacs when both she and Steel whipped their head to stare at a corner of the house.

A man strolled around the corner. He was tall with dirty-blond hair and the same cocky tilt to his lips Steel had. Except I had stopped thinking of Steel's expression as cocky or arrogant. He was observant. His mind was always working, but he wasn't thinking about how much better he was than everyone else. I wasn't sure about this guy. Though there was an air of familiarity with him because he was Venus's brother.

"Ronan," Steel greeted.

Ronan lifted his chin in a bro's way of saying hi. His green gaze slid to Brighton, and he cocked his brow. "I brought beer. You're old enough to drink, right?"

The tilt to his lips increased. He was teasing her. But Brighton's shoulders tensed. I couldn't see her face as she flipped burgers, but I imagined it was the same expression as when Steel had asked about Ronan earlier.

"I don't drink." Her tone was flat, unimpressed.

"More for me." Ronan took the five steps up to the patio in two leaps. His heavy boots thudded across the wooden patio. He lifted a bottle out of the bulky paper bag he carried. "Steel?"

Steel took the bottle. "Thanks."

I dropped to sit awkwardly in a folding chair. Ronan's gaze landed on me. His eyes were deeper green than his sister's, but his build was similar to hers. Only on him, it made his shoulders seem as wide as the house. Paired with the cocky expression and the shrewd gaze, he made an impression.

No wonder this guy intimidated Brighton.

Yet he gave me a pleasant grin as he took another

bottle out. "I hear you're not allowed to have any. Congratulations."

Surprised that not only did he seem friendly, but that he was making conversation with me, I smiled. "Thank you."

Juggling the rest of the six-pack in the crook of his arm, he ripped off the top of the beer and set a bottle of sparkling water on the ledge jutting out from the grill. Brighton scowled at it like she couldn't figure out what it was. He pulled out another drink for himself. "I didn't mean to announce that I was here, but when I drove through town and parked by Steel's pickup, half the diner came outside to stare at me."

Brighton snorted. "Were they all the females?"

"Always." He took a long pull and set the beer down on the porch railing. He reached into the brown paper bag again and pulled out another sparkling water. He handed it to me.

Surprised, I accepted it. Brighton had given me a bottle of water, but Ronan had gotten my favorite brand of mineral water. "Did you ask Venus what I liked?"

"Don't tell her I listened." He took the bag and slipped inside as if he owned the place. Which if everything worked out, it would be his house too.

He stopped and inspected the track, sliding the door back and forth as he determined what was making the squeaking noise. "This could use some—"

"You can set the table while you're in there." Brighton didn't bother looking away from the grill.

Ronan's answering grin was unrepented. Like a little boy who'd just discovered his parents' last nerve and couldn't wait to bounce on it. "Good idea. I can see if that needs to be fixed too."

I exchanged an amused glance with Steel. Being around these two made it seem like Steel and I had been together forever. I didn't know if Brighton and Ronan could get beyond their clashing egos, but they might have fun trying.

The rest of dinner went by quickly. Brighton finished the food, and we ate inside. Ronan bugged her about the house next door, wanting to know the owners, its age, how many families had lived there. As Steel and I snuck out, Ronan was arguing with her about fixing it up while he was here.

When we were outside, Steel threaded his fingers through mine. Walking through town, hand in hand, was more than nice. I could see us doing this in Silver Lake. Going for walks in the evening. Maybe I would get over my self-consciousness. I had made friends with Venus, and Ava had said she had been a notoriously hard person to get to know. Ronan had sounded the same, but after tonight, I could count him as a friend.

Yes, Silver Lake might turn out pretty well.

Steel's hot gaze brushed over my cheek. We shared a smile as we rounded the corner.

People were filtering out of the diner. I wanted to ask Steel if they had gathered to watch what happened with Ronan and Brighton, but I would save my question for when we were in the vehicle. No one needed to overhear us, and I wasn't sure exactly how good shifter hearing was.

Several pairs of eyes tracked us down the sidewalk toward Steel's pickup. I was squeezing his hand harder with each step, trying to appear casual.

I enjoyed my night, but I would be glad to leave. We

were on display, and my newfound confidence of not giving a shit what people thought wavered.

Two females sauntered across the street toward an old, faded-gray sedan parked a few spaces down from Steel's pickup. They studied me from head to toe. All the comments flooded back. I was a human, and I was mating one of their males. They abhorred weakness. I kept my head high, my chin up, but my grip was iron in Steel's.

He walked me around to open the passenger door. We were so close to ditching Garnet River.

"She's not even claimed," one of the females sneered.

Steel's muscles flinched under my grip. What did claimed mean?

The other female scoffed, her gaze unkind. "Can you blame him? I wouldn't want to claim a human if I was forced to mate them."

My hatred of mean girls had only grown over the years. I had been their target every year of my life. I had moved to another state because of them, and I was afraid of moving to Steel's hometown for this very reason. And even though this reaction was exactly what I had feared, the swift anger flooding my veins wasn't expected.

They didn't respect weakness. But they didn't respect me anyway. So what did I have to lose? "Are you salty because I'm human, or because he was here when he was single, and he was fucking me instead of either of you?"

The darker haired of the two women bared her teeth. I was surprised she didn't have fangs, but her cheekbones sharpened, and I wasn't imagining that she grew taller. When I had asked myself what the worst that could happen was, I had forgotten they could change into a creature four times my size.

A low growl resonated from Steel. He hadn't released my hand, and he tugged me closer to him. "You would do well to remember that not only is my mate pregnant, but I am a Silver. You've disrespected her, she retaliated. Anything further, and I will take it as a direct challenge to my family. And you will suffer the consequences."

A shiver raced down my spine. His tone was ice cold, and his threat was very real.

The female who had looked like she wanted to yank my tongue out of my mouth changed in a heartbeat. She was back to her human self, while her friend had gone pale.

Steel stared them down for a few more moments before he opened the passenger door and ushered me into the pickup. He closed the door with a slam and stalked to the driver's side.

I waited until he backed out and pulled away, his motions fluid and unhurried. He was displaying his power, showing the town he wasn't scared of them, especially not the two females who had insulted me.

Once we left the city limits, I asked, "What did she mean about claiming?"

CHAPTER
THIRTEEN

S teel

HER QUESTION WAS like storm clouds looming on the horizon. I hadn't talked to her about claiming. We were supposed to have time. But my gut told me she wouldn't be pleased with my lack of an explanation before she'd been publicly ridiculed for it.

"Shifters don't just mate. They can claim their mate."

"How?"

I could only hear her curiosity in her tone. Maybe my oversight wouldn't blow up in my face. "It's a bite. During sex, right at the peak for both. If a shifter takes a human mate, then the shifter does the bite. In shifter-only couples, sometimes it goes one way. It's very visceral... very innate and intuitive."

"I don't get it. What does it do that mating doesn't?"

This was where it could get touchy. I focused on her

scent, trying to separate out strong emotions, but it proved impossible. She was seemingly calm. "Mating does two things—it calms a shifter down and it provides oversight. The mates can watch out for each other. There is no living alone after thirty-five."

"That still doesn't answer what the difference is between claiming and mating."

This time I caught it. Her even, measured speech. She was protecting herself from her feelings until she learned all the information. There was nowhere to go but through. "Mating is mandatory, so some shifters have agreements."

A tiny line was forming between her brows that I wished I could smooth out. "It's like Ronan and Brighton? They could've agreed to mate, but they'd be nothing more than roommates?"

"Exactly."

A flare of hurt fizzled in the air, snuffing out her sweet peony scent. "So the bite is like a sign that the couple is really into each other?"

"Yes, but—"

"And you haven't claimed me."

"I wanted to wait—"

"Because you have to be with me. It just so happens we're compatible in bed, but I wasn't your choice."

"You are my choice, Avril."

Her expression turned guarded. "But you haven't claimed me. You haven't even told me what claiming is."

"Avril—"

"If those two hadn't pointed it out, you're saying you would've talked to me about it?"

"When I thought you were ready."

She circled her finger in the air. "And all the shifters,

everyone in Garnet River and in Silver Lake, know you haven't claimed me. They all think you're stuck with me."

I refrained from stomping on the brakes. I eased to the side of the road and stopped. "Avril, listen to me. You were having a rough adjustment, and I wanted to give you time."

"How much time? Like, after we did the whole mating thing, then say you claim me, would everyone think you just kinda got worn down?"

How could she think I felt like that about her? Hadn't I given her enough reason to trust me? "I don't give a shit what anyone thinks. You were my main concern."

"Answer the question, please." Her hurt clogged the cab. Fear. Regret. Anger. Her emotions were all over the place.

"I suppose people could think that. But I'm not worried about them."

She rubbed her temples and stared at the floor of the pickup. "I just don't know what to think, Steel. I had a really good time tonight. Then I heard that, and the explanation..." She hugged her arms around herself. "It doesn't help."

"I didn't mean to hurt you. We can go home, and I'll gladly claim you—"

Her derisive snort cut right through my chest. "Can we go home?" Resolution filled her voice. She wasn't going to talk more. She was shutting me out like she did two months ago. Like she tried to do when we were packing. "I'd like to keep talking about this."

Her gaze jumped to mine, and her glassy-eyed stare broke my heart. "Is there something else you haven't told me?"

"There's a lot about the shifter world we haven't covered."

Her lips pursed. "About us."

"I haven't hidden how I feel about you."

She cocked her head, confusion darkening the brown in her eyes. "How do you feel about me, Steel?"

"I asked you to come with me to Silver Lake because I wanted to be with you. And you know why I couldn't leave Silver Lake." I pinched the bridge of my nose. This might scare her off, but she had to know. "I would be thrilled about a baby—no matter what. But this baby is the best thing that's happened to me—because then I get you. When I said I've wanted you since I first saw you, I didn't just mean sexually. I wanted you to be mine. Mine and mine alone. It took every ounce of restraint not to rip that ex of yours apart. Because he got to touch you after I laid eyes on you. And when you turned me down? I was a shell of myself for months until Ava told me you were pregnant. So that's how I feel."

Her scent shut down. Only a lingering smell of peonies remained. She'd utterly closed herself off. *Fuck.* I should've kept my mouth shut. Her focus narrowed on me, as if she was studying me for an anatomy exam. What was she looking for?

As she came to a decision she wasn't going to share with me, she shifted her gaze out the window. "Please take me home."

Discussion over. Despair slowly crammed itself into every pore. I wouldn't hold her in the middle of nowhere against her will. I eased the pickup back onto the highway and the rest of the trip home was silent.

～

AVRIL

STEEL WAS INSIDE. The real estate agent had arrived and put the sign in the front yard. The place was officially for sale.

I perched on the front step. We hadn't talked since the car ride. We slept in the same bed but hadn't touched. I should be furious. Hurt. Appalled. But I kept getting stuck on his claims that he had lied to me while we'd been together.

My mind was a mess. My stomach wanted food. And my body wanted to be wrapped around him. But I had to sort a tangle of thoughts and emotions in my head.

The way those females had acted last night was humiliating. But that was the thing. It was like I had faced my worst nightmare—living the same life I had as a kid. I'd been determined not to let what they said or thought bother me. I had grown.

Then Steel had told me about the claiming bite. And I'd had to realize the base of my fear. That the man I fell totally and deeply in love with wouldn't love me back. Physically, mentally, emotionally, I was terrified he'd abandon me in any of those areas.

Then he'd made a helluva declaration.

And I was faced with getting what I desperately wanted.

Terrifying.

I wanted to cry. I wanted to rant. I wanted to rage. Why would I be scared of having a decent guy fall for me? One who couldn't leave and, by his actions, didn't want to? Why couldn't I be happy about it, settle down in Silver Lake, and live happily ever after?

I was fucked up, and I needed to figure out how to unfuck myself.

The condo was packed. The moving truck would be here soon. Then Steel and I were each going to drive our vehicles to Silver Lake.

As if my thoughts summoned the movers, a large white van pulled into the driveway. Steel came outside because, of course, he'd heard the deep rumble of the engine from blocks away.

"I'll take care of the movers. You can rest or get on the road." His gaze brushed over me for a moment, but I didn't look up. He shorted my thinking.

I was a shell of myself for months until Ava told me you were pregnant.

He'd been one-half of an empty shell while we'd been apart. I'd been the other.

I tapped my front tooth with a fingernail as I thought about the drive. Yeah, I would head out now. Go to my new life with a metric ton of baggage dragging from my shoulders.

I wanted a fresh start. A real fresh start. I didn't want to hide in Silver Lake. I wanted to enjoy my life. I had confronted a lot of my past. Except one major thing.

An idea formed in my head. My car was parked on the street to be out of the way. I strode to it and got in. Steel was in the garage with the two moving guys, gesturing and pointing as he gave them instructions for what needed to be moved.

Before I drove off, I shot him a message. **Thank you for handling the movers. I'm taking off.**

I didn't tell him my plans. I would have to wait until I knew I'd go through with it.

When I got outside the city and traffic on the interstate thinned, I considered my plan. I drove until I needed gas. Then I only stopped to put gas in and go to the bathroom. Before I left the gas station, I piled a hot dog and two burgers in my arms. They wouldn't be as good as Steel's food.

Steel. I wanted to call him. To tell him I was sorry I left so abruptly, but I had nothing new to tell him. I was a few hours from my destination. Then I could talk to him.

I munched on the bland, greasy food all the way to my hometown. It didn't stretch out in front of me in one shot. A gradual populating of buildings and businesses crowded the highway. I didn't have to go far. The trailer park I was heading to was on the edge of town.

I pulled to a stop in front of a familiar trailer. Time had not been kind, but it was in better condition than I had expected. I didn't get out for several moments. In the big picture window, a pail with flowers decorated the view. From where I was parked, I couldn't tell if they were fake or real. I wasn't even sure who lived here.

The lawn had been mowed, but it needed another clipping. Tears stung the backs of my eyes when I spotted the fluffy heads of pink peonies blooming by the porch.

I sniffled and climbed out. The flowers gave me courage. I walked through a four-foot iron gate that had been busted my entire life but was now neatly latched. The lump in my throat grew larger the closer I got to the front door.

Porch steps bowed as I climbed them. Planks of wood creaked under my feet as I approached the door. My hand was shaking when I knocked.

I didn't know who'd answer. My breath stalled as the dead bolt was flipped. The door opened to reveal a woman with thin salt-and-pepper hair pulled back from her face. Her face had thinned over the years, but there was a flush I hadn't seen for almost twenty years. A glow that I'd never seen before. Her eyes widened, and she covered her mouth with a hand.

"Hi, Mom. Can we talk?"

FOURTEEN

S teel

AVRIL HAD TAKEN OFF, leaving me to refrain from ripping the movers' throats out when they asked perfectly valid questions. I had hauled half of Avril's belongings to the truck while the two movers insisted I didn't have to help. But all that would've been left for me to do was prowl through her apartment like the caged beast that I was.

By the time her items were secured in the moving van and her condo was locked up, I sprinted to the pickup and hit the interstate. I wouldn't be able to catch up with her, but as long as I was closing the distance between us I could keep from losing my mind.

Was she even going to Silver Lake? She could be in fucking Wisconsin by now.

I'd like to think my gut would tell me if I was getting further away from her, that I would sense the growing distance between us, but if I could do that I wouldn't have epically messed things up.

I should've talked to her about the claiming. Told her I wanted nothing more than to sink my teeth into her neck. Yet that was exactly why I hadn't. She was already overwhelmed. It wasn't her fault or mine that she hadn't been given much time to adjust.

I stopped at the border between Minnesota and North Dakota, only because I had to fill up with gas. I hated taking the extra time. I glanced at my phone. My hope surged when I saw the missed message from her. All that was on it was an address. In her home-town. I had little idea what it meant. Had she gone there instead of my place? Did she want me to go there?

I should call her, but my fingers stalled over the screen. If she wanted to talk to me, she would've called. She hadn't even looked me in the eye when she told me she was leaving. She hadn't spoken to me. And I doubted she had looked back.

All I had was this address.

The good news was that she was heading in the direction of Silver Lake, nowhere near Wisconsin. So that was where I would head.

Each mile crawled by. Ninety minutes later, I was pulling up in front of an old trailer house. Yellow siding that had once been white lined the sides. Plywood was over one window that was most likely a bedroom.

I got out and took the narrow path to the door. The fence circling the lawn around the trailer sagged in several places and one stair was missing from the porch steps. Avril's car was parked directly in front. A twenty-year-old Corolla with the front fender hanging halfway off and rust chewing through the rims sat on the parking pad next to the trailer.

Whoever lived here had fallen on hard times long ago and hadn't been able to climb their way back up.

Unsure of what I was doing here, but suspecting this was Avril's childhood home, I leaped from the ground to the top of the porch, praying that the deck would hold my weight. Wood groaned but stayed solid. The whole trailer house rattled when I knocked on the door. Inside, I heard the low, growling voice of someone who'd trashed their vocal cords with cigarettes and alcohol over the years. Light footsteps with the same cadence as Avril's approached the door, and I waited, enshrouded in a cloud of stale cigarette smoke.

This place was an assault on my senses. I could hear the TV blaring in the trailer on the lot behind me. Engines roared up and down the main road, running in front of the trailer park. The smells weren't the fresh, unperfumed air I was used to.

Avril opened the door with an apologetic expression. "I'm so sorry I left without explaining. I didn't know what to say. I didn't know how this would go, or even if I had the guts to come all the way here."

Half my anxiety was wiped out by her apology. "Whatever you need, Avril."

She drew me inside to a tight entryway. A small stacked washer and dryer were at my right, and a wall was at my left. If I flared my elbows, I'd hit either one.

"It's also about what you need." She rested her hands on my chest. "I just had to get away to think. Because what happened in Garnet River bothered me, but I didn't know why. It didn't feel right to be upset with you, but I was, yet I wasn't."

"And you came home for answers?"

She touched my face, tenderness in her eyes. "This isn't my home. But I hoped coming here would help me be at peace in our home. Because I love you, Steel, and it's been extremely hard for me to accept that you might love me. It's terrifying, and it's been easier to assume you can't."

I cupped her chin. "I love you, I'm in love with you, I'm fucking crazy over you, Avril. What can I do to keep from scaring you?"

She brushed her hands down my arms, then turned, tangling her fingers with mine. "That was the thing. *You* couldn't do anything. You were already doing everything. I needed to figure my shit out, and this seemed like the best place to start." A smile ghosted over her lips. "And it's been good. I don't know if I would've been ready for this before you."

All the stress of the day drained away. "We've jumped the circle?"

"I've gone full circle so we can join ours." She rose to her tiptoes. I met her lips for a light kiss, aware there was someone on the other side of the wall.

Avril gave my fingers a squeeze and drew me behind her and around the corner. "Mom? This is Steel."

An older woman with tired eyes and thin black hair scattered with gray smiled at me from a little table by the big, drafty windows across from the kitchen counter.

"Ma'am." I didn't know her name. I knew this woman's story, and her daughter meant everything to me, but not her name.

Her knees were knobby in the thin gray sweats she wore as she rose and hobbled toward me. She had a cardigan wrapped tightly around her over a sweater. She was so thin, she had to be cold all the time.

Her hug was surprisingly strong, but I feared embracing her too hard and cracking her in half. "It's so nice to meet you. I feel like I should thank you for bringing my daughter back to me." She gave Avril an indulgent smile. "But I know it was Avril's decision. No one can make her do anything she doesn't want to."

Amusement traveled across Avril's face. "From now on, we'll be visiting regularly."

Tears glittered in her mom's eyes. "Seeing you again was one of the many things I wished for, but the only thing I never thought I would get." She blinked rapidly, fighting to keep her tears dammed. She waved her hands around her face and composed herself. "Anyway, call me Patti. Are you hungry? I just threw lasagna in the oven, but all I have to drink is water."

Avril exchanged a meaningful look with me. I put enough details together to figure out what she was telling me. Patti was sober. Since the smoke smell was stale, she'd also quit smoking. The trailer would forever smell like an old ashtray, but there were several signs around the interior that Patti had tried to maintain and update what was left of the place. A floral tablecloth lined the table. Every potholder and dish towel on the counter was decorated with humorous sayings. And from here, I could see the living room had a fairly fresh coat of paint.

I was grateful Avril returned to her hometown to reconcile with her past, but I would be eternally thankful she'd found her mother in a good place.

As Patti busied herself with pulling plates and glasses out of the cupboard, I slipped an arm around Avril's waist. "How long would you like to stay?"

"Are you okay if we don't leave right away tonight?"

"We'll stay as long as you need to. Deacon can meet the movers."

"You've promised to stay as long as needed before." The corner of her mouth tipped up and appreciation shone in her gaze. "Do you realize Penn said something similar when he came after Venus? That he was going to stay as long as he needed to? Is that a thing with the Silver brothers?"

"It's most definitely a thing." I pressed a kiss against her temple, wanting to touch her more, have her closer, but also satisfied just as we were.

I jumped to Patti's side to grab her armload. I took the plates and Avril retrieved the glasses from the counter.

Once the table was set, we sat around it while the lasagna finished cooking.

Patti folded her hands together and cast a pensive gaze down the hallway. "I'd love to offer you a place to stay, but I don't have a spare bed, and mine is really old and in rough shape."

"It's no problem. Point us toward the closest hotel, and we can meet for breakfast tomorrow too."

I'd do more than take her for breakfast. I had a tidy home. Unless she wanted to make big changes, we wouldn't need to do more than convert a room into a nursery. My hoard could go a long way for Patti, and I couldn't wait to talk to Avril about what we could do to help. What Patti would allow us to do.

Patti studied me more intently than I'd ever been scrutinized in my life. Finally, the intensity drained out of her gaze. "I think you got yourself a good one here, Avril. And trust me, I've been with enough bad ones to know."

I beamed like a schoolboy who'd been told he'd done

a good job helping in the classroom. This morning I thought I faced a future raising a kid with a roommate, but I had a mate I couldn't wait to claim and now her mom was part of the family too.

❧

AVRIL

I WALKED into Steel's house. My home. We'd spent a week with my mom. Deacon had the movers unload everything in Steel's garage, and we'd have unpacking to do. But that could wait.

Steel entered behind me, shutting us in.

"We're finally home," I murmured. Those words settled into my belly. Home. With the man I would mate in a month. We'd have our mating ceremony, and then his brothers, Ava, and Venus would come to my hometown and we'd celebrate with my mom and Ava's dad.

He brushed his hands up and down my arms, still behind me. "You're my dream come true."

I leaned my head back on his hard chest. "You're making mine come true." Being this close to him fired up all my hormones. My body tingled and warmth spread from where he was touching me and pooled between my legs. "Now, is it time for that bite?"

We'd waited. The hotel hadn't felt right, and he'd patiently waited. But I'd caught him eyeing my neck and now I had a new turn-on I hadn't known about.

"I never thought this moment would come," he growled.

162

I didn't know where we'd do it. Would he take me right here? On the couch? In the bed?

I didn't think it mattered where we were having sex when he claimed me, but it seemed to add a level of significance. We'd waited this long.

He took my hand and led me toward the living room and kept going. He bypassed the bedroom and went down the hall to the stairs. The attic room. We hadn't had sex up there yet.

My belly flipped in a million different directions as he stood at the bottom of the stairs and let me go up first.

When I reached the top, I stopped, my eyes going wide. "When did you get time to do this?"

The middle of the floor had been clear before, but now there was a plush steel-gray blanket with a few throw pillows. A vase of peonies sat in the window of the reading nook, but the petals scattered from the top of the stairs to the blanket were from deep-red roses. A wicker picnic basket was placed by the pillows.

"Steel? When did you have time to do this?" The drive hadn't been long, but we'd followed each other back and arrived at the same time.

"I called Ava. Told her I wanted to surprise you with a little something." He rubbed the back of his neck. "It's not much, but—"

He'd told me once he wasn't romantic, but he'd wanted to be for my claiming. I spun and grabbed his collar, hauling him toward me. I slammed a kiss on his lips. His arms banded around me and carried me to the blanket. I'd gotten used to being carried by my shifter. My legs were twined around his waist. When he lowered me to the pillows, he came down on top of me. I didn't let him go.

He broke the kiss to lick and nibble his way down my neck. I grasped the back of his shirt and tugged it over his head while he worked my shirt up. In less than a minute, we were both stripped down and he was entering me.

"I want to bury my head between your legs and feast, Avril," he grunted as he thrust inside. I knew the signs. This was going to be fast, rough, and thoroughly delicious. "But I can't wait to have you wear my bite."

"Do it, Steel."

He didn't take his time, and I didn't need it. We'd held back too long with each other. He stroked me to a swift peak and when I teetered at the top, he slid his hand between us. As soon as my climax slammed into me, rocking through me like I'd detonated, I naturally bared my neck.

He dipped his head and licked along my skin before he sank his teeth into my skin.

The sharp sting of pain magnified my pleasure until I was soaring. I went wild, bucking under him while he released inside me, his body rigid and pinning me down.

Finally, I collapsed, still cocooned by his big body. He slumped over me, kissing the spot he had bitten.

The slight throb at my neck matched the beat lingering between my thighs.

I was panting, trying to get my voice back after shouting God knew what. The neighbors might be able to tell me what I was yelling while he claimed me.

"That was amazing. It can only happen once?"

He chuckled, and it shook his body. He was still inside me, still hard, and he started moving his hips. I immediately matched his rhythm, circling my pelvis. "Honey, I'll bite you whenever you want." He dropped his head to kiss the other side of my neck and murmured, "Wherever you want."

I rolled my hips, taking him deeper. "Yes, let's do it there next."

"You're mine, Avril. All fucking mine."

EPILOGUE

S teel

I RUBBED a hand over my mate's growing belly and took in the room around me. We had converted the office into the nursery. There were three more months to go before the baby was born, but the crib and changing table were put together and in their spots. A bookshelf full of brightly colored books was against one wall, filled with books from my childhood and some from the attic reading nook. The other walls had vibrant paintings of dragons.

Mathilda had given us the name of a shifter who painted murals.

After I had explained the clan structure to Avril, and how the hues of the gems the clans were named after shimmered on the scales of the ruling families, Avril had insisted that one of each dragon decorated the wall. If the

Silvers were charged with overseeing the other clans, then she wanted our child to grow up knowing the importance of their position.

She leaned into my chest and hummed. "It turned out really nice. I can't wait to sit in the rocker and rock our baby to sleep."

"Me either." Even when I had first asked Avril to be with me as more than a rebound sex partner, I'd had no idea life could be this good.

Responding to my voice, the baby flipped, and I brushed my hand down her belly again as the baby rolled inside.

Avril put her hand on top of mine. "You two have a connection that would make me jealous if I wasn't so in love with you both."

"THERE'S no bond like a dragon shifter with its mama. Don't worry." I kissed the top of her head. "Speaking of mothers, how's her new house?"

"She's still nervous about it." Her voice was always laced with concern when she discussed Patti, but she loved having her mom in her life. "She has her garden mapped out, but I think a part of her will always feel like she doesn't deserve it."

I could've afforded any house Patti wanted, but Avril had anticipated her mother's conflicting emotions. When they discussed moving her to a place with decent insulation and air conditioning, Avril didn't fight her mom when she suggested another trailer. In the same lot where she knew her neighbors. The familiar was comfortable.

We took the same route with her car. Little by little, we offered repairs, using excuses like she needed a decent vehicle to come visit. It was a balance both of us were happy to strike as long as Patti stayed healthy and sober.

I continued rubbing her belly, knowing full well that keeping my hands on my mate this long usually ended up with me inside her. "Do you work today?"

"Mathilda said there're two females with checkups today. One's due in a month and the other is only a few months along."

Mathilda was both Avril's midwife and her mentor. She wasn't planning on retiring soon, but she and Avril agreed that more than one midwife for the shifter clans in this area was beneficial. My mate would shadow her until the baby was born, and if Avril liked the profession, she would enroll in the master's program.

"Do you have to leave for work right away?" she asked.

"I'll go out for a couple of hours, then work on my course." Penn had set me up with an online law school. I wasn't going for my law degree yet, not until after the baby was born and Avril was settled into her career, but I'd enjoyed the classes so far.

"I suppose we should go."

"Mmm." I swept her into my arms and carried her to our room. "We've got a few minutes yet."

WILL BRIGHTON SOFTEN TOWARD RONAN, and does he want her to in The Dragon's Pledge?

. . .

FOR NEW RELEASE UPDATES, chapter sneak peeks, and exclusive quarterly short stories, sign up for Marie's newsletter and receive my first wolf shifter story free.

About the Author

Marie Johnston writes paranormal and contemporary romance and has collected several awards in both genres. Before she was a writer, she was a microbiologist. Depending on the situation, she can be oddly unconcerned about germs or weirdly phobic. She's also a licensed medical technician and has worked as a public health microbiologist and as a lab tech in hospital and clinic labs. Marie's been a volunteer EMT, a college instructor, a security guard, a phlebotomist, a hotel clerk, and a coffee pourer in a bingo hall. All fodder for a writer!! She has four kids, an old cat, and a puppy that's bigger than half her kids.

mariejohnstonwriter.com

Follow me:

ALSO BY MARIE JOHNSTON

More in this series

The Dragon's Oath

The Dragon's Promise

The Dragon's Vow

Jade Dragon Shifter Brothers

The Dragon's Pledge

Want to try my very first shifter series?

<u>The Sigma Menace</u>

Fever Claim (Book 1)

Primal Claim (Book 2)

True Claim (Book 3)

Reclaim (Book 3.5)

Lawful Claim (Book 4)

Pure Claim (Book 5)

www.ingramcontent.com/pod-product-compliance
Lightning Source LLC
Chambersburg PA
CBHW030635190726
48286CB00008B/2532